OPER

235

THE RACE FOR URANIUM

Mike Drogemuller

OPERATION
235

THE RACE FOR URANIUM

Mike Drogemuller

Special thanks to my spouse and partner Jan, and our sons Seth and Will, for their encouragement to embark on this journey and their guidance along the way. To my dad Hugh, who is resting peacefully, and my mom Barb for encouraging my passion for history and politics, and to my brother Tony and sister Joanne for the great debates around the family dinner table. Many thanks to Liam Blackley for his editorial insights and assistance.

"In the course of the last four months, it has been made probable ... that it may become possible to set up a nuclear chain reaction in a large mass of uranium, by which mass amounts of power... would be generated. This new phenomenon would also lead to the construction of bombs, and it is conceivable that extremely powerful bombs of a new type may thus be constructed. Now it appears almost certain that this could be achieved in the immediate future.

The United States has only very poor ores of uranium in moderate quantities. There is some good ore in Canada and the former Czechoslovakia, while the most important source of uranium is Belgian Congo.

I understand that Germany has actually stopped the sale of uranium from the Czechoslovakian mines which she has taken over. That she should have taken such early action might perhaps be understood on the ground that the son of the German Undersecretary of State, von Wiezsacker, is attached to the Kaiser-Wilhelm-Institut in Berlin where some of the American work on uranium is now being repeated."

Letter to President Franklin Delano
Roosevelt from Albert Einstein
August 2, 1939

CONTENTS

PROLOGUE

I n March 1938, German scientists Otto Hahn, Lise Meitner, and Fritz Strassmann discovered the process of splitting the atom, the exothermic, or physical reaction required to develop an atomic weapon. The discovery set off a race between Germany and the West to conquer this potentially destructive technology. While the Germans were at the forefront of nuclear fission, the British and Americans were close behind.

In early August 1939, Albert Einstein, the most famous theoretical physicist of his age, wrote United States President Franklin Delano Roosevelt, alerting him to the threat posed by the German science and the potential of the energy source for the development of a super weapon. Einstein's advice was timely, as Hitler had already ordered his scientists to begin work on a nuclear bomb. However, Germany lacked access to the quantity of Uranium-235 required to turn the theory into a device.

The Germans were aggressive in attempting to source the required raw material. They spread their influence far and wide, however only a handful of nations mined the resource with Canada being the most significant producer.

Conquering Czechoslovakia gave the Nazis access to uranium, but not in sufficient quantities to build a bomb.

Through diplomatic channels, Germany let it be known to the operator of the Canadian uranium mine, at Great Bear Lake in the Northwest Territories, that it was seeking to purchase massive amounts of radium and uranium for 'scientific' purposes. Little was known about the uses for the minerals within the Canadian government and that was Hitler's advantage. Thus, theoretically there was no impediment to the Nazi state purchasing the ore.

1939 began with war in Europe brewing, as the Nazis stamped their authority on the continent. The British policy of appeasing Hitler was an abject failure, Victorian era military thinking dominated the leadership of many west European nations, and treaties limiting weapons production were ignored by the Nazis who by that year were on a full war footing. Germany had rebuilt its military industrial capabilities and was preparing to unleash its might on its European neighbours.

The United States could do little more than stand by and watch, as American politicians and their constituents had no stomach to participate in another European war. In 1939, the United States also lacked a military capable of exporting its power. In addition, the United States government did not have an intelligence network in place to keep an eye on its enemies or undertake operations out of the public limelight.

Against this background, this fictional account is written.

CHAPTER ONE

COMINGS AND GOINGS

MAY 1939

It was a beautiful spring day in Banff, Alberta, and Canadian Prime Minister William Lyon Mackenzie King was proudly escorting King George VI and Queen Elizabeth through the Rocky Mountains, as part of their year-long tour of Canada.

The Royal Couple were immensely popular in Canada and most Canadians, except for French-Canadian Quebecers, supported Great Britain and saw themselves as proud colonial subjects of the British Empire.

While the visit was a public relations exercise, it was also an opportunity for the two nations to do business. Canada was Great Britain's most important Commonwealth ally, and with war brewing in Europe, the

Brits needed as many friends as she could get. While the Prime Minister was showing the royal couple the sights of the Rocky Mountains, complete with a media entourage in tow, British High Commissioner, Sir Gerald Campbell, and Prime Minister King's Chief of Staff, Digby Summers, met to dust off some files.

Campbell and Summers enjoyed a good relationship and used the opportunity of following the Royals around to make some decisions that would solidify the British-Canadian relationship, to the disadvantage of Nazi Germany. Campbell was a very polished diplomat, having previously served as ambassador to the United States before taking on the Canadian posting.

The two met for tea in the lounge of the Banff Springs Hotel, a majestic property with sweeping views of the Rockies. They were discussing how the two countries could work together to curb Nazi Germany, given Canada's policy of not getting involved in a European conflict, the sole exception being an attack on British soil.

"You of course have our entire support, Sir Gerald, with the exception of putting boots on the ground on the continent," Summers said, putting his best spin on Canada's refusal to shed blood for its commonwealth parent.

"And we appreciate your government's support Digby, although I must admit that push may soon come to shove," Sir Gerald replied, steeling up to admit that the British government's policy of appeasing Hitler was a total failure.

Summers interjected, letting the ambassador off the hook. "Say no more Sir Gerald. Hitler has duped all of us. The question becomes what the Canadian government can do to help given our policy of not getting involved in a war in Europe."

Sir Gerald used the opportunity to background Summers on the situation surrounding nuclear energy, and the concern of his government that Nazi Germany was in the process of developing a super weapon.

"So, what you are telling me, if I have it correct Sir Gerald, is that the uranium at the Eldorado Mine should be banned for export with the exception of Great Britain and the United States," Summers said, having listened to Sir Gerald's summary.

"That is correct Digby," Campbell confirmed.

"According to our scientists, the Germans have developed technology that will enable them to produce a massive bomb, but they need substantial amounts of uranium to do it. All we are asking of the Canadian government is to place a trade ban on the resource until we have a better understanding of its destructive force," he continued.

"Ok Sir Gerald. I will talk to the Prime Minister. But I doubt he will have an issue if the goal is to prevent a global conflict," Summers replied.

And with that discussion, Nazi Germany's attempts to build its nuclear program using Canadian uranium were cut off at the knees.

AUGUST 1939

General Franz Halder summoned Admiral Wilhelm Canaris to an urgent meeting at the Reichstag, in Berlin, Germany's parliament building. Halder was Hitler's Chief of Staff while Canaris was head of the Abwehr, the German military intelligence service. Both were loyal servants of the Reich and veterans of the Great War.

Their meeting would be brief, as Halder was in the midst of planning for some major events, in addition to keeping his master Adolf Hitler under control, which was a 24-hour-a-day business.

The admiral was in his early fifties, tall, fit and with a full head of greying hair. He had been running the Abwehr since 1935 and had overseen its growth as the nation's key military intelligence agency. The Abwehr was established in 1920 with the initial purpose of defending the Fatherland against espionage from foreign governments. More recently, under Canaris' leadership, the agency had extended its influence beyond Germany's borders as it geared up to go to war with the rest of Europe. As conflict approached, the Abwehr faced increasing competition from Heinrich Himmler's Geheime Staatspolizei. Better known as the Gestapo, the secret branch of the German police was a more brutal version of the Abwehr.

It was a short distance from Abwehr headquarters to the Reichstag, so Canaris took the opportunity to enjoy the spring morning and walk to the meeting. When he arrived, he was cleared through security and escorted to Halder's inner office. The Chief of Staff's office was grand as befitting his title and position as gatekeeper to the Führer.

"Good morning, Willie," Halder said welcoming his old friend and military colleague with a warm smile. "It is good to see you as always."

"And you," Canaris replied saluting his superior and then extending his hand. Halder returned the salute, and the men shook hands.

"I would love to catch up Willie, but the Führer is running me ragged. I have another meeting in a few minutes, so I will get to the point," Halder said handing a folder to Canaris.

"Put this in your brief case Willie. They are your instructions for an important mission. It is top secret," Halder said firmly.

Canaris smiled empathetically at Halder, as he understood that life with Hitler was not easy. He opened his briefcase and deposited the file. "What do you need me to do Franz?" Canaris asked.

"All details are in the file Willie," Halder replied, "but briefly, I need you to get some intelligence resources to the Belgian Congo. Who you choose is up to you, but they will need to work independently and be able to take care of anyone who gets in their way."

"Now please excuse me," he said hastily. "I must get to my next meeting. I will walk with you."

The men left together and Canaris walked back to his office wondering what in the Belgian Congo was so important to the Führer, not daring to open the file until he was safely behind closed doors.

TWO WEEKS LATER

United States Consul to Belgium, Nash Owens, was getting ready for work. He was a Harvard graduate from a good east coast family and had visions of promotion up the ranks at the State Department. His family had the right connections to help fast track that process.

Brussels was his first posting, and his first time overseas, the only exception being a family fishing trip to a lodge in Nova Scotia when he was a teenager. Owens had joined the State Department straight after graduation three years earlier, passing the exams with ease and acing the interview process. The State Department loved Ivy League graduates. They had the 'right' breeding, excellent academic credentials, were well spoken, civilized, and able to take care of themselves in the rough and tumble of the cocktail circuit, where diplomatic business was done.

Owens had been posted to Brussels six months earlier. As consul, he managed the administrative duties at the embassy. Like most juniors in the foreign service, he was trusted with the routine aspects of embassy life, such as issuing passports and visas. The political functions would come later once he had proved himself.

The slim, five-foot ten-inch diplomat had curly black hair and brown eyes. He was ironing a white business shirt while standing in his socks and underwear. His three-piece tailored suit hung over a mannequin and his brief case rested on a chair next to the door of his room. Owens was fussy and fastidious. A crease in the wrong spot on his shirt would ruin his day.

There was a knock at the door. "Yes?" Owens called to the person interrupting his morning routine.

"Will you be having breakfast this morning Mr. Owens?" The person at the door was Owens' land lady Mrs. Van Houk. A short elderly woman, with a pot belly and matching backside, she liked to mother Owens, much to his irritation.

"I will be there in a minute Mrs. Van Houk," he replied patiently as he focused on getting the last crease out of his button-down shirt.

"Why don't you let me do your ironing Mr. Owens? I have time during the day." She asked, knowing the diplomat's morning routine, and trying to be helpful as she also knew her tenant struggled with the chore. Owens bit his tongue, resisting the urge to tell his landlady to mind her business. He was determined to have a perfect crease.

He finished getting dressed, choosing a red and gold striped silk tie to complement the navy suit, and a matching red handkerchief for his breast pocket. He picked up his briefcase and went downstairs for breakfast. Mrs. Van Houk was waiting for him as he sat down at the breakfast table. She poured him a cup of coffee and shortly thereafter brought him a typical European breakfast of a pastry, rye bread, a hardboiled egg, cured meat, butter and cheese.

He thanked her and put his nose into yesterday's Times of London. The newspaper was delivered each day to the United States embassy courtesy of the British Foreign Office. He took it home with him every evening once the ambassador and his superiors had finished reading the day's news.

He loved routine almost as much as his bespoke suits, which were a gift from his parents and made for him by a tailor on Savile Row in London, the fashion hub for well to do gentlemen on the continent. He had ordered three and wore them on alternating days, never missing a rotation. On every other Saturday morning he turned the Friday suit over to the dry cleaner so that it would be cleaned and pressed in time to meet his rigid fashion schedule.

Unfortunately, Owens was not entitled to a private residence until he had been promoted a few rungs up the diplomatic ladder. So, he had to make do with the quaint boarding house, or shell out his own funds for a private apartment—which he was loath to do on his modest wage.

The headlines reported the grilling Prime Minister Neville Chamberlain had received in Parliament, during question period, over his failure to curb Nazi Germany. Labour and Conservative politicians alike were getting their boots into their embattled leader.

Looking at his watch it was 8 a.m. and time for him to depart the boarding house for the short walk to the embassy. Owens liked to leave for work at precisely the same time every day. It was a wet summer morning in Brussels, so he picked up his umbrella and put on an overcoat.

* * *

Later that morning, Belgian Mining Corporation president Edgar Sangier walked through the front door of the United States embassy, nodded at the military guard, and approached the reception desk. Sangier was dressed in a three-piece grey suit. He was wearing a raincoat and carried a brief case and umbrella. Sangier was middle aged, balding, and bespectacled. He was slightly overweight for his five-foot nine-inch frame.

The friendly American receptionist greeted Sangier. "May I help you?"

"I have an appointment with Mr. Owens. My name is Sangier," he replied courteously. Sangier had initially sought a meeting with the ambassador, however he was not deemed important enough to warrant a hearing with the senior diplomat, so was shuffled down to Owens.

Looking at her diary she saw the meeting was on the day's calendar. "Oh, yes Mr. Sangier. Please go through and up the stairs to the second floor. Mr. Owens' office is third on your left."

She pointed to the door behind her desk where a marine was standing guard. Sangier thanked the receptionist and proceeded through the door and up the stairs. He entered the outer office and was greeted by Owens' secretary.

"Good morning. You must be Mr. Sangier. Mr. Owens is expecting you. Please go through," she said cheerfully.

Sangier smiled at the charming young American woman and entered Owens' office. Owens was sitting at his desk going through a growing list of passport applications, as anyone that could was trying to leave Europe.

"Mr. Sangier. Good morning." Owens stood and offered his hand.

Shaking Owens' hand Sangier replied. "Please call me Edgar."

Owens gestured to a chair next to his desk. "Please sit down. How can I help you Mr. Sangier?"

Sangier took a seat and got to the point. "I have something the Nazis want, and I need your help to keep them from getting it."

Frowning, Owens responded. "We are not at war with Germany, Mr. Sangier."

"It is just a matter of time Mr. Owens. Hitler has already invaded Czechoslovakia. It is just the beginning," Sangier replied fatalistically.

In textbook recitation, Owens gave Sangier the official foreign policy line of the US government. "Be that as it may the United States government is officially neutral on European affairs. But what help do you need from my government Mr. Sangier?" he added, encouraging Sangier to get to the point.

"I own a mining company Mr. Owens. The Belgium Congo Mining Corporation. We have important mineral deposits in the Congo. The mineral in question could change the nature of any future conflict."

Speculating, Owens asked, "And which mineral are we talking about? Gold, diamonds?"

"Uranium, Mr. Owens. Have you heard of it?" Sangier replied.

Shaking his head Owens admitted, "I am afraid not. I studied law at Harvard, not geology," ensuring his Ivey League pedigree was dropped appropriately on Sangier.

Sangier continued. "Uranium is the fuel for nuclear energy Mr. Owens. This energy can be used for peaceful means—to generate electricity—or for military means—to make a bomb such that mankind has never seen. A bomb so powerful that a city like New York or Washington could be reduced to ashes in seconds."

"Surely you are being melodramatic Mr. Sangier," Owens replied skeptically.

Looking grim, Sangier said. "I can assure you I am serious Mr. Owens. If the uranium falls into the wrong hands, it will change the course of the war we are not yet fighting. You need to understand Mr. Owens the German government is much further advanced than any western country in harnessing the potential of nuclear energy," he continued. "Their scientific discovery, called nuclear fission, gives the Nazi's a military advantage that the West cannot compete with. Fortunately, the Germans do not yet have access to a large source of uranium, so they need to buy it from another country. Aside from the Congo the other country mining substantial quantities uranium is Canada, and the Canadians will not sell it to the Nazis, for good reason." Sangier said, completing the briefing.

Sensing that Sangier was not trying to game the system for a United States passport, and telling the truth without exaggeration, Owens moved the discussion forward. "Very well Mr. Sangier. How can the United States government help?"

Sangier opened his brief case and pulled out a file.

"Two things Mr. Owens. First, a ship containing uranium is leaving the Congo today. The shipping documents show her destination as Antwerp. She is in fact going to New York. I need that shipment safeguarded upon its arrival and consigned to the United States' government. I also need your help getting the rest of the uranium safely out of the Belgian Congo before the Germans seize it," Sangier said.

He handed Owens a file containing copies of shipping documents, letters to the manager of the mine and local port manager confirming his instructions, relevant details of the mine for the United States government, including the title of ownership, a map of the Belgian Congo marked to show where the mine was located including travel routes from Leopoldville, and a geological survey and description of the resource.

Glancing at the documents Owens said, "Ok Mr. Sangier. I will get instructions from the State Department and be in touch."

"Don't wait too long Mr. Owens. If the Nazis get the uranium, there will be no need to go to war. It will be over before it begins."

Sangier hesitated. "There is one more issue, Mr. Owens."

"What is it?"

"A car has been passing my house regularly. It slows down and stops across the road, and the two men in it seem intent on watching me come and go. My guess is they are German agents," Sangier said.

After a brief pause, he continued. "I am not paranoid, Mr. Owens."

Nodding, Owens said. "Okay Mr. Sangier. I believe you. I will do my best to help. How can I contact you?"

He handed Owens a business card. "Call me any time. Day or night. The details are on my card."

Owens reached into his desk drawer and reciprocated with his own card. The men stood and shook hands as the meeting concluded.

"Good day Mr. Sangier," Owens said as the Belgian left his office.

Owens picked up the phone and called Lieutenant Commander Dean Butler, the embassy's military attaché. Butler was also on his first posting and both men were good friends despite having quite different backgrounds and personalities. They had been posted to Brussels on the same rotation and both being new to the city, and Europe, spent much of their free time together, exploring the sites of the city and the surrounding countryside.

The young officer graduated near top of his class at the Naval Academy in 1935. Prior to that he had completed basic training with the marine corps and applied to Annapolis upon the recommendation of the camp commander. He spent three years serving on destroyers before being promoted to his current position.

Butler was also a country boy who had grown up on a dairy farm near Albany, New York. He loved the outdoors, particularly hunting and fishing. His parents and older brother ran the family farm, but the men in the family had always served their country in times of war. Butler's father was a Lieutenant in the Great War, and a graduate of the New York Military Academy. He retired from the army to take on the farm from his own father and raise a family.

Butler was gregarious, cavalier, and willing to take risks. However, the posting in Belgium was too tame for his liking. The Belgians had a small military, supported by vintage Great War armaments. The nation would be incapable of fighting a conflict with Germany without the help of neighboring allies France and Holland. He also did not particularly enjoy the dinners and cocktail parties he was obliged to attend. Socializing and small talk were not his strong points.

He did however like the freedom that came with the posting. He took every opportunity to visit Belgian military facilities, mainly as an excuse to get out of the embassy and go hunting and fishing in the eastern region of the small nation, which was heavily forested and sparsely populated.

Butler was sitting at his desk cleaning his shotgun, having spent the previous weekend in the Ardennes forest shooting pheasants and pigeons. He put the weapon down to answer the phone. "Good morning. Butler speaking."

"Good morning, Dean," Owens replied.

Recognizing Owens' voice, Butler said, "Hey buddy, what's going on?"

"Have you got a minute?" Owens said sounding concerned.

"Sounds serious. Did you break your iron again?" Butler replied chuckling at his own humor.

"What do you know about uranium?" Owens asked ignoring the dig about his fastidious nature.

Butler rifled around his disorganized desk looking for a communique. "Give me a minute." He searched unsuccessfully for the piece of yellow paper.

Speaking quickly, he summarized what he knew. "Knox has a bee in his bonnet about it. The President as well. Department of Defense sent a communique to all embassies a few weeks ago. I have a copy here somewhere," he said still searching his desk. "I gather a scientist named Einstein wound up the brass about it. Something to do with nuclear energy whatever that is. Uranium is like the gas that drives the motor from what I understand. Except the motor is a v-three million not your standard block-eight. Does that make sense?"

"It does. I just met with the owner of the Belgian Congo Mining Corporation. He wants to turn his entire uranium resource over to the United States government. He has a ship leaving today from the Congo loaded with it. I have a copy of the shipping documents. The paperwork shows the freighter is going to Antwerp, but he has instructed the local staff to reroute it to New York," Owens said completing the circle.

"Interesting," Butler replied vaguely, not really comprehending the gravity of the situation.

Owens continued. "There's more. He is convinced the Nazis are going to seize the mine and wants the United States government's help to get the rest of the uranium on a ship and out of harm's way. If they get hold of the uranium, he thinks the Nazis will build a bomb with it and wipe out a good chunk of Europe, or worse, Washington or New York."

"Explains why the brass are concerned," Butler replied seriously, the penny dropping.

"You better send a message to State and ask them what they would like us, or you, to do," Butler said placing an emphasis on 'you.'

"Fancy a beer after work?"

"Sounds good," Owens replied. "Let's meet at the Commonwealth Club at five. See if we can pick up some gossip from the Brits. I will cable State now."

"Ok. Later buddy." Butler hung up and continued to search his desk for the missing document.

* * *

It was early afternoon, the same day, in the Belgian Congo. The ocean freighter Augustus was birthed at the port of Matadi, the furthest inland port from the Atlantic Ocean. Matadi was several kilometres up the Congo River from the river mouth. The 4,700-kilometre-long river served as the principal thoroughfare through the vast country, and the port was the life blood for importing and exporting goods to sustain the emerging nation.

Thanks to Belgian colonial rule the river was dredged sufficiently to accommodate ocean going freighters. Matadi was discovered by British explorer Lord Stanley sixty years earlier, in 1879, as he trekked inland to discover the whereabouts of his missing colleague Dr. David Livingstone. It was serviced by a road and railway line to Leopoldville, the nation's capital, which was further inland.

Ahead of the Augustus' departure, the captain of the freighter was meeting with the port manager to sign off on the paperwork.

The captain did not like the Congo and was happy to share his disdain with anyone that would listen to his grumbling. The port manager, Henri Goma, was a cheerful black man who was used to the captain's gnarly temperament as the Augustus was a regular visitor.

Goma made his way up the gangplank. He had a sly smile on his face as he watched Captain Frits Van Hoeven yell at a dock worker to hurry up and fill the ship's diesel tanks.

"Good day Henri. Here is the paperwork," the captain grumped as he handed over the shipping bill of lading.

Goma took the paperwork from the captain and quickly glanced at it. It was the same shipment as always and the only deviation to the freight bill was the shipping tonnage.

"We will be underway within the hour. Is all the paperwork in order?" Van Hoeven asked.

Nodding, Goma gave the paperwork back to the captain. "All is good Frits. Please sign here and here," he said, pointing at the relevant signature lines on the document, which Van Hoeven duly signed.

"Have a safe trip Frits," Goma said pleasantly, concluding the formal business. He took the top copy of the freight bill with him and left the carbon copies with the captain for presentation to the customs authority in Antwerp.

"Thanks Henri. I cannot get out of here fast enough," Van Hoeven said, hoping this would be his last voyage to the African continent.

Goma departed the Augustus and walked slowly back to his office, enjoying the sunshine and the light breeze coming off the ocean several kilometres to the west.

A short while later a mud-covered truck drove up to the wharf. Thomas De Suter, site manager of the Belgian Congo Mining Corporation got out and walked briskly up the Augustus' gangplank. He was carrying an envelope. "Are you ready to sail captain?" De Suter asked as he walked along the main deck towards Van Hoeven.

Shaking hands with the Belgian Van Hoeven replied, "Yes Thomas. We will be underway as soon as the lazy shits on the dock finish filling the tanks. What brings you here?"

Handing the envelope to the grumpy dutchman, De Suter said, "Instructions for you from Edgar. Do not open them until you are well clear of port."

Van Hoeven gave De Suter a quizzical look. "Sounds intriguing. What do they say?"

"Do as you are told captain and open them when you are well clear of port." De Suter replied sternly. "Now I must get to the mine. See you when you return."

Ignoring the schoolmarm attitude, Van Hoeven replied, "Hopefully, this is my last trip, Thomas. I hate this place."

Nodding sympathetically, De Suter said, "We have another load to get ready and time is of the essence. Safe passage." De Suter departed the ship and started the long drive back to Shinkolobwe.

* * *

Later that afternoon, a Lufthansa Airlines Focker-Wulf Fw 200 Condor was disembarking passengers down portable stairs at Leopoldville Airport. The four engine Condor was the flagship of the fleet. It had entered service the year before in 1938 and could fly more than 5,000 kilometres non-stop.

Named after Belgian King Leopold, Leopoldville was the colonial capital of the Belgian Congo. The local Congolese were forced to serve their relatively recent imperialist conquerors, who were busy plundering the natural resources of the mineral-rich colony. The Belgians had received the Congo as compensation for being on the right side of the Great War. The previous German landlords were evicted from their colonial holdings, having been forced to pay compensation for the misfortune of losing the conflict.

In the arrivals terminal, which was no more than a shack with a coat of paint and an iron roof, a man was holding a sign. His name was Christian Schmidt, and he was the German consular official tasked with picking up VIPs from the airport. He was there to collect a man named Hofmayer. He did not know anything about the visitor, only that he was required to provide anything the man needed during his stay.

A fat man climbed down the stairs and pointed at Schmidt seeing the sign with his name on it. He rudely pushed past another passenger who was walking too slowly for his liking. Schmidt would try to be helpful because he knew Hofmayer was an important visitor, and few Germans came through the previous colony these days.

Seeing Hofmayer point at him, he snapped to attention and made the Nazi salute. "Herr Hofmayer? Sieg heil! My name is Schmidt. I am from the German embassy."

Hofmayer ignored the formalities and simply nodded at Schmidt. "Is it always this hot?"

Schmidt replied earnestly, "You will get used to it once you have been here long enough."

Hofmayer was visibly irritated by the heat, wiping his sweating brow with a handkerchief. "In that case you will need to find me comfortable quarters because I do not plan to be in this horrible place a moment longer than is needed."

Looking pleased with himself Schmidt said, "Of course. All is arranged. I have booked you into the finest hotel, the King Leopold. May I ask how long you plan to be in Leopoldville?"

"That depends on how fast you can arrange to get me to Shinkolobwe. I have business there," Hofmayer said directly.

Schmidt replied, "Of course, I will make the necessary arrangements. My superiors in Berlin did not advise me of any details of your visit."

"You had no need to know," Hofmayer snorted with an air of superiority. "Arrange transport for me immediately.

I also need a list of all ships leaving the country in the last week."

"I will go to the port in the morning, Herr Hofmayer," Schmidt replied. They got into the embassy's Mercedes and drove off.

CHAPTER TWO

SHOW AND TELL

The Commonwealth Club in Brussels was a members-only establishment. It housed a bar, lounge and restaurant and had guest rooms for members who needed a discrete place to stay. It was located on embassy row near the Royal Palace. Ex-pats, diplomats, spies, businessmen and journalists frequented the club. It was a busy establishment, and discussions inevitably revolved around Nazi Germany and its intentions towards its European neighbours.

Owens spotted Butler standing at the bar and joined him there. "Hi Nash. Any news?"

"Got a message from State telling me to standby for instructions," Owens replied to his colleague.

"At least someone at State is working," Butler said cynically. "What are you having?"

Owens pointed at the beer taps. "Stella thanks."

Butler signaled to the bartender and pointed at the Stella tap. The bartender poured a glass of beer and slid it to Owens.

"Shall we get a table?" Owens suggested.

"I am good standing. I can see what is going on. Unless of course you insist," Butler teased knowing from experience that Owens would insist they sit.

Owens predictably insisted causing the naval officer to smirk.

They sat down at a table near the bar and continued their discussion. "What do you think State will do with this Belgian mining chap?" Butler mused.

"I don't know but my best guess is they will want him in the US," Owens speculated. "That communique you dropped off earlier suggests nuclear power is a hot potato." Looking around the club Owens spied a familiar face entering the bar. "Ah. Look who has arrived," he said pointing his head in the direction of a tall well-dressed gentleman. Owens waved to the man who walked over to join the Americans.

"Who's that?" Butler asked.

"Nigel Parker-Biggs," Owens replied. "Number two at the British embassy. Rumor has it he runs the Secret Intelligence Service desk."

British SIS agent Nigel Parker-Biggs was a smooth-talking Oxford-type with an understated sense of humor. Like the Americans he was in his late twenties. Biggs was tall and good-looking and also wore bespoke suits hand made by a Savile Row tailor, albeit with wider pinstripes. The SIS was more commonly known as MI-6.

Owens stood up to greet Biggs. They shook hands. "How are you Biggs? Please join us," Owens said cheerfully. Owens was pleased that one of his British colleagues had turned up, meaning he would not be shut out on gossip that evening.

"Thanks, old boy," Biggs replied politely, with an accent suggesting he had enjoyed a privileged upbringing. Turning to Butler, Biggs did the introductions. "I do not believe we have met."

Butler stood and shook hands with Biggs. "Lieutenant Commander Dean Butler. Pleased to meet you. I am military attaché at the embassy."

"Would you like a drink Biggs?" Owens offered, gesturing to the waiter.

"Thank you, Owens," Biggs replied as the waiter arrived at the table. "A sherry please, old man."

"Another round gentlemen?" The waiter asked directing his attention to Owens and Butler.

"Please," Owens confirmed. The waiter went to the bar to fill the men's glasses.

"How's business Biggs?" Owens asked inquisitively.

"Getting ready for war, or so it appears," the spy replied nonchalantly.

Owens nodded. "It does seem inevitable. Chamberlain is taking a pounding in the House and the press. What does the Foreign Office think?" Owens asked, knowing that British politicians were all over the map on how to deal with Nazi Germany.

Biggs' voice took on a more serious tone. "Officially we are supporting Chamberlain's appeasement strategy. Unofficially, we think this will only give Hitler more time to make his next move. And if that happens, then Chamberlain, as they say, will be snookered. Hitler's actions in Czechoslovakia turned more than a few heads in Cabinet and the Prime Minister seems to be growing a spine finally. So, we shall see," he concluded doubtfully, not convinced that the Prime Minister and Cabinet had what it took to deal with Hitler.

Owens nodded. "That is State's view as well."

He paused and then got to the point of the gossip session. "What do you know about uranium, Biggs?"

"Not a lot except that it is a very sensitive topic at the Foreign Office," Biggs replied casually, suggesting he knew quite a lot about the subject.

"A team of physicists at the University of Birmingham are working on the science and have cabinet level access." He volunteered, throwing a piece of information on the table. "Why do you ask?"

"I had an interesting meeting today with the owner of a uranium mine in the Belgian Congo. He wants to turn over the entire production of his mine to the United States. He thinks the Nazis will take it if we do not move quickly," Owens said, recounting the discussion with Sangier earlier in the day.

The waiter delivered the drinks.

Biggs pursed his lips, put the fortified wine to his nose to enjoy the caramel flavours, then swirled the liquor in the small flute shaped glass, as he mused on the subject. "That is interesting. What is State going to do?" He asked evenly after the brief pause.

"I don't know yet, but I expect we will help out," Owens said. "Nuclear energy is a big deal with President

Roosevelt. Can you find out the lay of the land on your side?"

"Happy to Owens," Biggs replied with a sly smile. "But only if we play show and tell as they say."

Owens readily agreed to share any information he found out with Biggs, as the Americans had no spy network operating in Europe.

"I will call you when State gives me directions." Owens continued, wanting Biggs to know that the matter was going up the chain of command at the State Department.

"I am sorry to be rude gentlemen, but my appointment has just arrived." Biggs said. A middle-aged gentleman had entered the club and nodded at the British spy. Biggs' tone made it clear to the Americans that the matter was not social, and they were not invited. "I will be in touch. Cheerio." Biggs got up and moved to the table where his appointment had taken a seat.

"Who's that?" Butler asked Owens, interested to know who Biggs was meeting with.

"I don't know unfortunately," Owens replied. After looking at how well the man was dressed, he opined, "Probably a diplomat or businessman of some description. He is too well dressed to be a journalist."

Moving back to the uranium discussion Butler observed, "Sounds to me like the Brits are all over this and Biggs knows more than he is letting on."

Owens agreed. "I expect so. Biggs is very resourceful, and I think we will need his help. I cannot imagine the Nazis will roll over on this one."

* * *

Bill Donovan was reading the New York Times and waiting to have dinner with his wife and two children in their Upper East Side Manhattan apartment. Donovan was a veteran of the Great War, an attorney, and former United States deputy attorney general. He had also retained his standing in the army as a reservist with the rank of Major General. Despite being a Republican, he was a close confidante of President Roosevelt and helped the government from time to time.

Betsy Donovan called from the kitchen. "Kids, Bill, dinner is ready. Everyone sit up at the dining table."

Two young children made their way into the dining room. They were dressed in private school uniforms. Donovan sat at the head of the table having finished reading the day's news.

"How was your day, kids? What did you do at school?" Donovan asked his children.

Billy Junior looking disinterested, replied, "Nothing."

His young daughter Tess, tried harder to impress. "Our teacher took us to Central Park, and we learned about nature."

The telephone rang. Donovan looked at Tess. "Hold that thought." He patted the children on their heads as he retreated to the living room. The phone rang for a second time, and he answered. "Good evening. Donovan speaking."

"Bill. Frank Knox here." Knox was an admiral, head of the Navy, and President Roosevelt's chief military advisor on global security issues.

"Hi Frank. How are things?" Donovan asked knowing full well that the phone call was not social. Knox only called when there was a problem.

"Fighting fires as usual Bill," Knox replied bluntly. "I need you in DC tomorrow. The Navy will pick you up. Be at La Guardia at 7 a.m. sharp." Knox promptly hung up.

Donovan returned to the dinner table. "Was that Frank Knox honey? What did he want?" Betsy asked.

Donovan replied. "Don't know honey but something is up because the Navy is picking me up at La Guardia first thing in the morning."

His wife sighed. "Whenever he calls you disappear somewhere. I will pack you a bag for all seasons."

"Thanks honey," he said holding her hand. "Sorry kids, daddy has to go away for a few days." The kids looked sad as their father was heading out on yet another adventure for the government. This usually meant that he would be out of their lives for a prolonged period.

"I will get back as fast as I can," Donovan acknowledged sympathetically, seeing the looks of disappointment on the faces of his family members.

* * *

German agent Max Kuplow arrived unannounced at Sangier's office the next morning. Kuplow was a large, humourless man. He stood almost six foot four inches high and weighed at least 250 pounds. He was wearing a black three-piece suit and a black leather overcoat. He had the classic Aryan features of blond hair and blue eyes and a stern demeanor which belied his attempt to be pleasant.

Kuplow knocked on the outer office door and let himself in. "Good morning. Can I help you?" Sangier's secretary, looking surprised then fearful, asked the behemoth German.

"Good morning fräulein. Is Mr. Sangier in? There is a matter I wish to discuss with him," Kuplow said.

"Do you have an appointment Mr...?"

"Kuplow," he interrupted. "I represent the German Commodities Import Company. The matter is urgent." Kuplow in fact worked for Canaris at Abwehr. The admiral had decided to attack the uranium problem on multiple fronts, including via a commercial transaction. Kuplow was there to purchase the ore and money would be no object.

Nodding, the secretary replied, "One moment. I will see if he has time to see you."

"Thank you Fräulein," Kuplow said, feigning grace.

The receptionist knocked on the door and entered Sangier's office. Sangier was sitting at his desk putting together a second document folder for the Americans.

"Mr. Sangier? A Mr. Kuplow is here to see you. He says the matter is urgent," the now frightened secretary informed Sangier.

"Did he say what he wants?" Sangier asked frowning.

"No. Only that the matter is urgent," she replied, then hesitated and grimaced. "He is German Mr. Sangier."

"Hmm. Please show him in," Sangier replied with concern. He quickly put the file folder in the desk drawer.

Sangier's receptionist invited Kuplow into his office. "Mr. Sangier will see you Mr. Kuplow. Please go through."

"Thank you fräulein," he said with a forced smile, trying unsuccessfully to be nice.

Sangier swallowed nervously as the big German entered his office. He knew this would at best be a difficult discussion. At worse, potentially violent.

"Good morning Mr. Kuplow. Please take a seat. How may I be of assistance?" Sangier asked neutrally, trying to hide his fear of the big man, and knowing the Germans were actively watching he and his family.

"I represent a German commodities company. My business card Mr. Sangier." Kuplow sat down and handed Sangier his card. "I will get to the point Mr. Sangier. We would like to purchase twenty tons of uranium from your mine in the Congo."

Sangier took a deep breath, knowing his answer would not satisfy the German. "I am afraid I cannot help you at this time Mr. Kuplow," said Sangier factually, albeit a bit meekly. Collecting himself and looking at Kuplow, he said vaguely but truthfully, "All our production is committed to other customers."

"Perhaps you can come back in six months when we have additional production available. Alternatively, I can put you in touch with a Canadian mining company who I believe have considerable supply available," he suggested, trying to move the problem elsewhere.

"My company would be prepared to take delivery on a staggered basis," Kuplow said, trying to be reasonable, which was not his nature. "We can take the ore in smaller lots."

"And price will not be an issue Herr Sangier," he added, hoping that greed would persuade the Belgian.

"I am sorry Mr. Kuplow. As I said, we really do not have any production available right now," Sangier said digging his heels in, doubting that the German was anything more than a front man for the Nazi regime.

"We could supply you with that amount of radium." Sangier said, trying to appear to be both helpful and ignorant to Germany's intentions for the uranium. "The minerals have similar properties."

"No, we must have uranium, Herr Sangier." Kuplow said firmly, now frustrated by Sangier's stonewalling.

Seeing the discussion was going nowhere, Kuplow stood up and leaned menacingly over the desk, putting his face less than an inch from Sangier's.

"You do not understand Herr Sangier," he snarled. "We will have the uranium, one way or the other. We have many ways to obtain it. Do you understand me?"

Now scared and knowing Kuplow would not take no for an answer, Sangier conceded out of fear for his own safety and that of his secretary and family.

"In that case Mr. Kuplow, let me see what can be done. We will need to move some customers to accommodate you." The Belgian conceded nervously.

Kuplow stepped back from the desk and sat down, smiling at Sangier, and assuming naively, that his thuggery had the desired effect. "I am pleased you have decided to be cooperative Mr. Sangier."

Trying to stall, Sangier lied to Kuplow. "I will need time to draw up the contract Mr. Kuplow. Please come back in the morning at 11 a.m. and I will have the paperwork prepared."

"Very good Mr. Sangier. See that you do. For your own sake," Kuplow warned menacingly. To reinforce the threat, the German picked up an orange that was sitting on Sangier's desk and crushed it with his huge fist, splattering juice all over the desk. "I will see myself out Herr Sangier, and I will be back tomorrow morning at eleven to complete the contract."

He turned and left the office, wiping his hand with a handkerchief.

Sangier's receptionist rushed into his office having locked the outer office door. "Who was that man Mr. Sangier? He frightened me."

"Me as well," Sangier said taking a deep breath and trying to shake the feeling that he had just escaped a potentially life-threatening encounter. "Get the American embassy on the phone please Gretchen. I need to speak to Mr. Owens," he said as he closed the door behind his secretary and slumped into his office chair, taking off his glasses and rubbing his eyes to try and relieve the tension he was feeling.

Sangier's secretary immediately called the embassy and was connected to Owens' office. The diplomat's secretary answered and put the call straight through. "Good morning. Nash Owens speaking."

"One moment, Mr. Owens," the miner's secretary said. "I will get Mr. Sangier on the line."

"It is Edgar Sangier, Mr. Owens," Sangier said with a shaky voice. "I just had a German businessman in my office threatening me if I did not sell him the uranium. I am sure he is a Nazi agent Mr. Owens." Sangier continued, his hands still shaking from the encounter.

"Take a deep breath Mr. Sangier and tell me what he said." Owens asked the Belgian, trying to calm him down upon hearing the fear in his voice.

"That if I did not sell him the uranium, he would acquire it one way or another."

"What did you tell him?"

Sangier summarized what he had told Kuplow. "There is one more thing Mr. Owens. The men that I told you about yesterday are continuing to park across the road from my house."

"Ok Mr. Sangier," Owens said making up his mind, despite not having a direction from the State Department. "This is getting dangerous, and we need to get you and your family to safety. We cannot allow the sale of the uranium to the Germans."

"Have you heard from your superiors in Washington?" Sangier asked.

"Only that I should stand by for further instructions. Please stay by your phone and I will call you back in fifteen minutes. Ask your receptionist to run an errand and make sure the German has left the building," Owens said out of concern for Sangier.

Owens hung up and immediately called Butler. "Can you come to my office Dean?"

"Sure. What is up?" Butler asked.

"I will tell you when you get here," Owens replied with a serious tone in his voice.

"On my way buddy." Butler hung up and jogged down the hall to Owens' office, sensing a crisis was brewing.

"Ok. What's up Nash?" he said as he barged into Owens' office.

"A German businessman just turned up at Sangier's office and threatened him if he didn't sell the Germans the uranium."

"Abwehr or Gestapo probably. Nasty types," Butler speculated. "What did Sangier tell him?"

"He told him to come back tomorrow morning once he had prepared the contract. So, we need to get Sangier and his family out of Brussels before then. He also said there is a car watching his house from across the street."

"Do you want my help with the thugs in the car?" Butler volunteered, showing enthusiasm for the anticipated task.

"Yes, and then get the Sangiers to the airport," said Owens, explaining that he would also need to look after Sangier's wife and two children.

"Consider it done," Butler confirmed.

"Do it in the morning before Sangier would normally go to work. Remember we are not at war with Germany, Dean. Just get the agents out of the way." Owens warned his gung-ho colleague.

"Aye, aye Nash," Butler said, faking a salute as he left the office.

Owens opened his desk drawer and pulled out a flight schedule for Belgium's national airline, Sabena. He scanned it quickly and then picked up the phone to call Sangier and provide details of the escape plan.

"Mr. Sangier please. He is expecting my call."

Sangier's secretary did as she was told and Sangier immediately picked up the phone. "Yes, Mr. Owens."

"There is a flight to London tomorrow at 10 a.m.," Owens said to Sangier as he got straight to the point. "We are going to get you and your family on it. We will take care of the agents watching your house. Be ready at 8 a.m. One of my men will drive you."

"What are your family members' names so I can get the tickets organised."

Relieved, Sangier provided his family's details then concluded the discussion. "Thank you, Mr. Owens. We owe you a great debt. What will you do about Kuplow?"

"Leave Kuplow to me Mr. Sangier. Just have your family ready by eight in the morning," he said hanging up the phone. He got up from his desk. It was time to brief the ambassador.

* * *

Donovan landed at Washington-Hoover Airport at 9 a.m. the same morning. The United States east coast was six hours behind Belgium. Knox was waiting in a naval limousine as Donovan walked down the stairs of the C-47 transport, the military version of the DC3.

"Good morning, Bill. Good flight?" Knox asked shaking Donovan's hand as he got out of the car to greet his colleague.

"Bumpy as always Frank. What is going on?" Donovan said directly, knowing there must be a national security issue brewing.

"I will brief you on the ride in," Knox said, "We are meeting with President Roosevelt and Secretary of State Hull in a half hour."

Donovan let out a quiet whistle wondering what he was in for.

Knox and Donovan were on time and ushered through White House security to the Oval Office in the West Wing.

Seated in a wheelchair at his desk, President Roosevelt cheerfully greeted both men. "Welcome gentlemen, please take a seat." The men sat down on the couch opposite Secretary of State Cordell Hull.

"Do you know Cordell, Bill?" Roosevelt asked, making the introductions.

Donovan replied, "We have not met. Pleased to meet you Mr. Hull." The two men shook hands.

"Likewise, Bill. Please call me Cordell. The President has told me good things about you." Hull replied. "I read your report on Ethiopia. It was very thorough."

The President got straight to business. "Cordell, please update Frank and Bill on the latest."

Hull took over the discussion.

"Bill, I gather Frank briefed you on the way in from the airport," Hull queried.

"Yes, he has given me the basics of the situation," Donovan said with a neutral tone in his voice.

"The Nazis are doing their best to get the uranium, one way or another," Hull continued. "The mine owner was threatened by a Nazi agent according to our man in Brussels."

Knox interjected. "What is State going to do Cordell? This is your project." Knox wanted to be sure everyone knew that it was a State Department matter, and the military was there to lend a hand as required.

Hull continued. "We are going to get the Sangiers to safety. Edgar Sangier is the mine owner. Nash Owens, our consul in Brussels is making the arrangements. Your military attaché, Lt Commander Butler, is giving him a hand. I have instructed the ambassador to lend all resources as required."

"The bigger issue gentlemen is securing the uranium," Roosevelt said. "From what I understand Sangier has re-routed a shipment to New York. We need to make sure it arrives safely. Frank, can you get a destroyer to the west coast of Africa to track down the freighter and escort her to safety?"

"Consider it done Mr. President. We have assets in the region," Knox replied in a businesslike fashion.

The President continued. "Bill, I need you to go to the Belgian Congo and make sure we get the rest of the deposit out safely. We have no one down there but we will get the British to help. It is our operation Bill, so do not let the Brits push you around. Why don't you take Owens and Butler with you? They are across the operation and might be useful."

Donovan nodded and looking concerned, asked, "Are we expecting opposition sir?"

"We need to assume the Germans will have agents in country Bill," the President warned. "Frank will get the Navy to send a destroyer and a freighter to get the uranium out. Getting it to the port will be your job."

"Yes sir," Donovan said, confirming his commitment.

Hull spoke up again. "From what we understand the Germans are well ahead of ourselves, the Brits and their Europeans allies in the development of a nuclear program. Their issue however is a lack of uranium. Specifically, the 235 derivative. I met with the Canadian ambassador yesterday as our neighbors to the north are also mining uranium, but nothing close to the purity of the resource in the Congo," he continued. "He said the Germans had been trying to purchase uranium from a Canadian mine, but the government kiboshed export sales to the Nazis at the request of the Brits."

"Ok gentlemen," Roosevelt said winding up the discussion. "I will leave it to you to work out the details. Remember, we are not at war with Germany, and I do not want to start one," the President warned, knowing the politics were against him currently. The American public and both houses of Congress were dead against the United States getting involved in another war in Europe.

Knox reassured the Commander-in-Chief. "Yes Mr. President. Bill let's go back to my office to work out the details."

"Very good. God speed gentlemen," President Roosevelt said, ending the meeting. Roosevelt's meetings and correspondence with Professor Einstein had been both fascinating and dire, meaning this issue had his full attention. "Cordell, come back and see me when your plans are in place," Roosevelt ordered. "I want to let Chamberlain know what is going on. Not that it will matter. For a politician that man has no nose for politics."

"Yes, Mr. President," Hull replied smiling at his boss' perfectly accurate assessment of the embattled British Prime Minister.

The meeting ended and Donovan, Knox, and Hull exited the Oval Office. They discussed the details of the plan while walking down the hall of the West Wing.

"This could get dangerous Frank. Are the two the boys in Brussels up to it?" Donovan asked, expressing his concern about working with two diplomatic types.

"Butler is, I don't know Owens. Dean is Frank Butler's son. If he is anything like his father, he likes the rough and tumble. I was in the Great War with his father. Butler junior is an academy graduate, and did basics in the marines, so he can look after himself," Knox said doing his best to provide Donovan with comfort that he would not be hung out to dry.

"Owens is a Harvard-type but quite resourceful and I have been impressed with his management of the situation with the Sangier's. I am confident that you will be able to count on him in a fight Bill," Hull said backing his charge, albeit with less conviction, knowing that Harvard graduates lived by their brains and not their brawn.

Knox turned to Donovan, "We'll get you on the Clipper to England Bill. You can pick up a flight from there to Lisbon."

"Cordell, can you get Owens and Butler on their way to Lisbon. The embassy in Lisbon will make the arrangements to get the three of you to the Congo. Can you also give the Brits a heads up that we might need their help on the ground?"

"I will see to it Frank," Hull confirmed.

"Let's get back to the office Bill, and get you on your way," Knox said to Donovan as they climbed into the waiting Navy Cadillac.

CHAPTER THREE

NOT AT WAR

In Leopoldville, Schmidt phoned Hofmayer to inform him that he had made arrangements to get him to the mine. Hofmayer was in bed with a local girl.

"Hofmayer speaking," he said with a distinctive German accent.

"Herr Hofmayer? This is Schmidt from the embassy, can you speak?"

"Yes. Have you made the arrangements?"

"I have arranged for our head of security to pick you up first thing in the morning. It will take most of the day to get to the mine."

"And the shipping information?" Hofmayer reminded Schmidt.

"I have a list of all ships leaving port over the last week, as well as the freight they were carrying. A small payment to the port master took care of what you required." Schmidt replied sounding pleased with himself.

"Good. Get the information to Admiral Canaris immediately," the spy instructed.

"At once Herr Hofmayer. Captain Meyer will pick you up at 6 a.m. It is a dangerous place you are going to," Schmidt warned the spy.

Fobbing off the cautionary note Hofmayer retorted arrogantly, "I am more than capable of looking after myself Herr Schmidt."

Hofmayer hung up the phone and then looked coldly at the girl in his bed.

"Get out, I have things to do," he commanded rudely, throwing the young woman her clothes. The girl got dressed and left his room.

* * *

Butler was dropped off by an embassy car a few blocks from the Sangiers' house. He was wearing an overcoat concealing a custom-made Griffin & Howe pump action shotgun. The weapon was from the young sailor's personal collection, and it was his favorite piece. Butler was a keen hunter and the Griffin had been put to good use shooting pheasants and pigeons in the Belgian countryside.

He walked casually along the sidewalk as if on an early morning stroll and stopped next to a Mercedes sedan parked across the street from Sangier's house. Two men were in the car, and they fit the descriptions provided by Sangier. They were both large and well-built, and more than capable of looking after themselves. Butler tapped on the driver's side window with his shotgun, immediately getting their attention.

"Put your hands on the dashboard and don't make me use this!" Butler commanded aggressively, waving the shotgun at the two men. The shocked looks on their faces confirmed they had been taken totally by surprise.

"What is this?" The driver cried out in a German accent.

"Shut up and do as you are told!" Butler said coldly, again waving his shotgun. The men yielded and put their hands on the dash of the Mercedes.

Butler pointed his shotgun at the driver. "You, get out of the car slowly and put both your hands on the hood!" he said firmly. The driver slowly exited the Merc following Butler's order to the 'T.'

Pointing at the passenger, Butler commanded, "Now it is your turn, Fritz. Hands on the hood. Very slowly so I do not have to use this." He again waved the shotgun to demonstrate he was serious. The passenger followed Butler's order believing that the American would make good on his threats.

Butler frisked both spies, removing handguns they were concealing as well as taking their wallets and identity papers. "Hans, get into the bushes and put your hands on the tree. Fritz stay where you are, or I will blow your fucking brains out!" He hissed quietly.

Pointing at a tree surrounded by bushes several feet behind the sidewalk, he commanded the men to move off the street and into the bushes to conceal them from passing pedestrians. The driver moved to the tree placed his hands around the trunk and Butler handcuffed him so that he was hugging the tree.

"Your turn Fritz." Butler commanded.

The passenger turned around, but rather than walking into the bushes, he swung wildly and violently at Butler, catching the young officer with a glancing blow to the ribs. Butler grimaced in pain, and was knocked off balance, but regained his composure in time to avoid a left hook from the big German. The young naval officer sidestepped the blow and countered with his shotgun, slamming the butt into the Nazi's stomach, winding the German who doubled over from the painful blow. Butler then slammed the butt into the man's jaw, knocking him to the ground and leaving him unconscious, with a broken jaw, missing teeth and blood streaming from his mouth.

Butler dragged the man by his shirt collar into the bushes then handcuffed him to the same tree as his colleague. He took a moment to collect himself and rub his sore ribs, quickly concluding that no serious damage had been done. He set about finishing the task of disabling the German agents.

"Your shoes gentlemen." Butler chuckled, now enjoying the moment and thinking about the total humiliation he was subjecting the Nazi spies to. Butler removed the men's shoes and threw them further into the bush. Finally, he gagged both with handkerchiefs and rope.

"Don't go anywhere." Butler smiled, knowing the spies were now helpless. The agent he had knocked out was still unconscious but breathing normally. He got into the car, drove it around the corner and parked in front of a row of expensive looking town houses. He opened the hood and removed the distributor cap. He then slashed each tire with a large knife. A neighbor came out of his house wondering what was going on.

With his best Flemish accent Butler said, "Good day sir. I am with the Mercedes Benz automobile company. We are evaluating our service standards. A truck will be here shortly to fix the car."

The neighbor shrugged and went back into his house. Butler turned the corner, crossed the street, and knocked on the Sangiers' door. Edgar Sangier opened the door straight away and let Butler in.

Butler introduced himself. "Mr. Sangier, I am Dean Butler from the American embassy. I have taken care of your friends across the street. Are you ready?"

"I watched and yes, we are ready," a visibly relieved Sangier confirmed.

"Are you alright?" he asked Butler, having witnessed the fight a few minutes earlier.

"I will survive Mr. Sangier. Nothing serious."

"But we had better leave before your neighbors call the police," Butler said, now nervous that he might have gone too far.

Not wasting any time, Sangier, his wife, and their two children loaded their luggage into the trunk of the family car, then climbed inside as Butler took the wheel.

"Do you need directions to the aerodrome?" Sangier asked.

Butler replied, "I know the way. Owens is meeting us there with your travel documents. You will be on the flight to London at 10 a.m. From there the embassy in London will arrange to get you to the United States."

* * *

Owens paced nervously outside the departure terminal at the Brussels Aerodrome as he waited for Butler. He was relieved as a car pulled up and the Sangiers got out, followed by Butler. This was his first operation, and the young diplomat was well out of his comfort zone. The spy game was vastly more dangerous than the droll routine of rubber-stamping passport applications.

"Any problems Dean?" Owens asked nervously, aware that his career would be ruined if there was an incident with Nazi Germany on his watch.

"Piece of cake. They will be out of action for a while," Butler said nonchalantly not wanting to mention to Owens his sore ribs, knowing his partner would worry unnecessarily.

Turning to Sangier, Owens handed him the airline tickets. "Here are your travel documents Mr. Sangier," Owens said. "Once you get to London you will be met by our embassy staff. They will arrange United States passports and passage to New York. A State Department representative will meet you in New York."

"We are in your debt Mr. Owens, and yours as well Mr. Butler. What will you do about Kuplow when he arrives at my office?" Sangier asked, still concerned that the German spy would cause trouble.

"The Belgian police are going to pick him up. Apparently, there have been several burglaries in that neighborhood and Kuplow fits the description of the perpetrator. They will release him in twenty-four hours," Owens replied, silently patting himself on the back for hatching a cunning plan to sideline the big Nazi.

Kissing Owens on both cheeks, a tearful Mrs. Sangier gushed, "Thank you, Mr. Owens. Our lives are in your hands. Bless you."

"You will be safe now Mrs. Sangier and tomorrow you will be United States citizens," Owens said stoically, regaining his composure following the awkward public display of affection. "Your flight leaves shortly. You better go through and check in. Goodbye Mr. Sangier and thank you for your service to the United States of America."

"Thank you and goodbye Mr. Owens. I hope we will meet again when this is all over," Sangier said. They shook hands and the Sangier family disappeared into the terminal.

"You didn't hurt the Nazis I hope?" Owens asked his partner still concerned that Butler might have gone too far.

"Nah. Left them tied to a tree. Someone will let them loose eventually," Butler laughed. "I was more concerned that the police would turn up and ruin the party."

"Good. Now we need to get to Lisbon," Owens said as he briefed Butler on their travel plans. "State says we will be meeting a man named Bill Donovan. He is leaving New York today and should arrive in Lisbon the day after tomorrow. Pack your tropical gear Dean, we are going to the Congo to make sure the uranium gets out safely."

"Roger that. Who is Donovan?" Butler asked.

"Fixer for the President," Owens replied. "Most of his file is need to know, so he is obviously an important cog in Roosevelt's inner circle," Owens continued, impressing upon Butler the political importance of their new commander.

Butler nodded thinking that if he was the President's man, then he would be up to the task. "Ok. When do we leave?"

"The flight is at two o'clock. I will give you a lift back to the embassy," Owens replied. They got into a waiting car and drove off.

* * *

Back in New York, Donovan was readying himself for the trans-Atlantic journey courtesy of Pan-American's Yankee Clipper. The sea plane had made its maiden run from New York to Southampton, in England, several weeks earlier. With stops in New Brunswick, Newfoundland, and Ireland, the flight was a cattle run. He would eventually arrive in Lisbon courtesy of an Empire Airways flight from London's Croydon airport.

The Clipper's first-class experience was hardly a burden. The Boeing 314 flying boat had three dozen births and cruised at three hundred kilometres per hour. In-flight amenities included reclining seats that converted into bunks, separate men's and women's changing rooms, and a silver service restaurant and lounge, where four-star chefs and white-gloved waiters looked after the passengers.

The Clipper would overnight in Gander, Newfoundland at a luxury hotel custom-built for the airline. It was the start of the romantic era of aviation and Betsy Donovan was slightly put off that her husband would enjoy the experience in her absence. For Donovan however, the thought of another jaunt to a remote part of the world was not an enticing one, but he had a job to do and little time to prepare. A glass of Chateau Lafite Rothschild accompanied by Beef Wellington was little comfort for the tropical afflictions like malaria, typhus, and diarrhea that would inevitably follow him on his forthcoming adventure.

Back in New York, and with little time available, Donovan was able to meet with theoretical physicists Robert Oppenheimer and Albert Einstein who were working in a lab at Columbia University on the Upper West side. The scientists were well advanced in perfecting their own process for achieving nuclear fission.

After the crash course in nuclear physics Donovan went to Argosy Bookstore, on East 59th Street, near his own home, to pick up a map of the Congo and reading material courtesy of the exploits of Stanley and Livingstone late the previous century.

The United States lacked a foreign intelligence service in the 1930s and had little influence over affairs in Africa, as France, England, Portugal, Belgium, and Italy ruled the roost in that part of the colonial world. Germany had been kicked off the continent after the First World War, as the Treaty of Versailles forcibly divorced the nation of its colonial wealth. Fortunately, its ally Italy, courtesy of fascist dictator Benito Mussolini, was happy to function as Germany's proxy in Africa.

Finally, Donovan went to his doctor to pick up a prescription of chloroquine to combat malaria, as well as diarrhea remedies to ward off the maladies that he was likely to encounter during his time in the equatorial African nation.

He was as prepared as he could be as he boarded the Yankee Clipper at Port Washington on Long Island. The Clipper roared down the bay and took off northwards over the East River, in the direction of its first stop in New Brunswick almost 1200 kilometres away.

* * *

Back in Washington, Secretary of State Cordell Hull returned to the White House to brief the President now that the plans were in place, and the would-be spies were in transit to their destination.

Hull was sitting on the sofa while Roosevelt sat in his wheelchair. It was getting late, so the President took the opportunity to pour Hull a twenty-year-old Talisker single malt, which had recently arrived courtesy of British Prime Minister Neville Chamberlain.

"Well Cordell," President Roosevelt started, "I don't know if we are ready to jump in the deep end or not."

"That makes two of us Mr. President," Hull agreed. "I think the Brits have a good ground game though, and as long as Chamberlain stays out of the way, we might win the day."

"Cordell," President Roosevelt said, thinking aloud, "We are going to need a dedicated organization to do these kinds of jobs in the future. We both know that war is on the way, and the American public are dead against us getting involved, but if we are going to get dragged into a fight, I want to be ready," he said looking seriously at Hull, who he knew was both a pragmatist and a hawk, particularly with respect to Hitler.

"What do you have in mind Mr. President?" Hull asked, wondering where the President was heading with the discussion.

"I want to have an intelligence capability like the Brits with their SIS. The Nazis obviously have their own spies," President Roosevelt said getting to the point. "I want to be ready Cordell, but there is no way Congress will go along with the idea right now, so it must be a function that can be kept discretely away from our friends-on-the-hill's scrutiny. That means such a capability could only be resourced through the Office of the President," he concluded. "What do you think?"

"I think it's a good idea sir and long overdue," Hull replied supporting his President. "There is no way we would get funding from Congress to run an intelligence service through the State Department, particularly if the House and Senate knew it was advancing our efforts to be ready for war."

"My thinking exactly Cordell," President Roosevelt said, pleased that Hull knew the pitfalls of dealing with the pre-war American Congress and its right-wing isolationists.

"I think when Donovan is back from Africa, I will invite the two of you in for a chat," he concluded having already made his choice of chief spy.

Hull agreed and they both sipped their single malts knowing that the world was going to hell in a hand basket, and the United States of America was far from ready for the maelstrom that would follow.

* * *

Patrolling off the West African coast, German submarine U-073 was searching for the Augustus. The captain and executive officer were on the conning tower deck peering through their binoculars at empty ocean.

U-073 was a long-range submarine on its maiden cruise, having been launched in February 1939 and passing its sea trials twelve weeks later. The Nazi government was precluded from manufacturing submarines under the terms of the Treaty of Versailles, but Hitler quite happily thumbed his nose at the other signatories, as he pressed for a comprehensive military advantage on the European continent and beyond.

The submarine's patrol route was supposed to take her into the Mediterranean where she would refuel and take on provisions at the Italian port of Naples. From there she would patrol the Mediterranean, playing cat-and-mouse with the British and French navies to evaluate her stealth. When she docked in Naples, she was ordered to the West African coast.

"What do you think Schneider?" Captain Jaanzen asked, wanting input from his executive officer. "There is no sign of the Augustus. We should have found her by now," Jaanzen said trying to find a solution to their search pattern.

Schneider replied, "Perhaps we should move north captain. She might have gotten further than we thought."

Jaanzen mused on the notion that the Augustus had got past them but dismissed the thought. "I do not think so Schneider. She is an old freighter and I doubt she makes more than seven or eight knots when she is fully loaded."

Tapping his fingers subconsciously on the guard rail as he thought through the problem, he theorized, "What if she is not going to Antwerp as the paperwork says?"

Schneider considered Jaanzen's theory for a moment then replied, "In that case she will probably make for North or South America. If so, she will be further west and probably a bit south if she is as slow as you think she is."

Jaanzen agreed with his young officer, slowly nodding his head as he considered the possibilities. "It is possible she is heading for Brazil or Argentina, but if so, the question is why?"

He continued his thought process subconsciously pulling on his beard as he worked through the problem. "What would motivate a captain, carrying uranium ore, to defect to Brazil or Argentina? And if she were ordered to go there by her mining bosses, who would they sell the product to?"

Schneider shook his head. "There really doesn't seem to be any point given the cargo."

"On the other hand, in America there would be many potential customers," Jaanzen concluded. "So, I think it is more likely she is heading to the east coast of the United States."

"Then we need to move west southwest," Schneider said confirming the captain's own thoughts.

Jaanzen thumped his hand on the rail of the conning tower. "Give the order Schneider. We need to find this needle in a haystack." Schneider left the conning tower platform and slid down the ladder onto the bridge.

To get the most speed out of the submarine, Jaanzen decided to stay on the surface where they could make seventeen or eighteen knots, at least twice the speed of the Augustus. If she were on her way to America, the Germans would run her down.

CHAPTER FOUR

CAT AND MOUSE

O wens and Butler were on board a Sabena airlines DC3, bound for Lisbon. The flight would take about five hours. The twin turbo-prop's top speed was three hundred kilometres per hour, and they had about 1,500 kilometres to travel. The airplane tilted sharply uphill from bottom to top and was narrow, with twin seats on either side of the aisle. The interior was well appointed and offered generous leg room for the eighteen passengers on the flight.

Shortly after takeoff, Owens updated Butler on the State Department's instructions. "I had a communiqué from State, Dean. We are meeting Donovan at the Estoril Hotel in Lisbon and the embassy is booking our passage to Leopoldville, capital of the Belgian Congo. Donovan should arrive in Lisbon in the next twenty-four hours."

"What about our British friends? Any word from Parker-Biggs?" Butler asked.

Owens replied, "No, but the Brits have agreed to help as required. Hull cabled the embassy in London, and the ambassador arranged for Lord Halifax, the British Foreign Secretary, to instruct the Foreign Office to provide all necessary aid."

"Good. Any sign of bad guys down there?" Butler asked.

"Nothing yet but the Brits are going to do a bit of reconnaissance. We will know more when we get there," Owens replied.

"So where is the mine exactly Nash?" Butler enquired trying to put together a mental map of the mission.

"From what I understand it is a few hundred kilometres southeast of Leopoldville, and there is a dirt road as well as a train link to the mine. It is near a town called Shinkolobwe," Owens explained. "Sangier put a map into the document package, but I haven't had a chance to look at it yet."

Owens took his briefcase down from the luggage rack above. He took the map out of the document folder and gave it to Butler to study.

A stewardess arrived shortly after with a trolley of canapes, caviar and a bottle of champagne. The attractive Sabena airlines stewardess leaned over her trolley. "Can I offer you refreshments and hors d'oeuvres before dinner gentlemen?" She asked, smiling courteously.

"Yes please, I am famished," Butler said, showing more interest in the food than the attractive woman preparing the plate.

"A glass of champagne and beluga caviar please," Owens asked enthusiastically, showing off his State

Department breeding and command of the finer things in life.

Smiling at the handsome and polite Americans, the stewardess poured a generous glass of vintage Bollinger champagne for both and prepared a plate of hors d'oeuvres for Butler who took no time devouring the snack. Owens was also pleased to receive a good-sized helping of beluga caviar. Reading the menu tucked into the seat pocket, Butler was excited about the prospect of having Steak Diane for dinner. The Navy, as well as the Army, marched on its stomach.

* * *

It was dawn in the Congo, and Hofmayer was standing outside the King Leopold Hotel, waiting for his ride to the mine. The hotel had been built in honor of the Belgian monarch a few years earlier and naturally was a five-star property. He scowled at the sight of a Belgian colonial police car doing the rounds of Leopoldville, mindful that he was in enemy territory.

A Wehrmacht captain and sergeant pulled up in the hotel's driveway. Both were attached to the German embassy's security detail. The soldiers were not in uniform, choosing to wear safari outfits to make it look like they were on a hunting trip. They were driving a Volkswagen Kübelwagen, the German version of the American jeep that would become the staple ride of the allied forces a few years later. It was loaded with supplies, and both were carrying hunting rifles and wearing side arms.

The captain approached Hofmayer, the only white man standing outside the hotel entrance. "Herr Hofmayer?"

he asked, speaking with a slight German accent. Hofmayer nodded affirmatively. "I am Captain Meyer of the Wehrmacht. I am head of security at the embassy. This is Sergeant Fischer. We are your guides in this ungodly country," Meyer confirmed.

Hofmayer nodded, again getting straight to the point. "Very good. How long is the drive to the mine?"

"Five or six hours depending on the state of the road," Meyer replied. "We have brought provisions. I do not think we will be able to get there and back today."

"Good. Let's get moving," Hofmayer said as he squeezed his large girth into the back seat of the Kübelwagen.

Meyer handed Hofmayer a high-powered rifle with a scope and a box of ammunition. "You might need this Herr Hofmayer. It is not the two-legged animals about which I am concerned." Hofmayer took the rifle looking pleased with the quality of the weapon.

* * *

Owens and Butler arrived in Lisbon later that evening and were having a drink at the bar of the Estoril Hotel. The Palacio Estoril as it was formally known was the most luxurious hotel in Lisbon, having opened several years earlier in 1930.

Butler looked around at the plush surroundings, impressed with the mahogany joinery and dark burgundy Indian marble floors with matching columns. Fresh flowers adorned the reception area, and the sofas and wingback chairs in the lobby were hand made and covered with dark chocolate leather and red velvet upholstery.

"You guys at State do it in style Nash," he remarked. "If we were on the Navy plan, we would be bunking in the single officers' quarters, eating at the canteen and doing our own laundry."

Owens concurred. "Enjoy it while you can Dean. I doubt the Congo will be this comfortable."

Butler asked, "So how do we get there exactly? The Congo is literally the middle of nowhere."

Owens replied, "The embassy is dealing with it, but Sabena and Air France have flights to Africa from here. It shouldn't be too difficult notwithstanding the Congo could not be more remote of a location to operate a mission."

"It would be easier if we were picking up the uranium at the South Pole," he said facetiously, reinforcing his point.

Butler agreed but was not overly interested with the administrative details of the mission. He was happy to leave the organization to Owens. "Look what the cat dragged in partner." Butler said nudging Owens, as he waved at Parker-Biggs who was walking through the front doors of the hotel.

Nigel Parker-Biggs looked around the hotel lobby and walked straight to the bar once he spotted the gregarious American waving at him.

"Gentlemen. So, we meet again."

The men shook hands.

"I take it this isn't a coincidence Biggs," Owens retorted.

Biggs smiled. "Your Secretary of State asked the Foreign Office to give you a hand and quite helpfully provided me with your itinerary. So here I am. In any event, Jerry is active in Lisbon. It is a neutral port, and all sorts of characters make their way through here. So, we like to keep an eye on things."

"A dry sherry please barman." Biggs asked, catching the eye of the bartender who acknowledged his order with a nod.

Butler scowled. "Great. Why couldn't we find another country to transit through?"

"I am afraid old boy, that Lisbon is also the jump-off point for Africa. One of the benefits of neutrality," Biggs replied. "And until Franco is overthrown, I am afraid Spain is out of bounds."

He spotted an attractive woman entering the hotel and his smile immediately evaporated.

"Speaking of spies. One of our friends from the Abwehr has just arrived," Biggs said, forcing a smile. He pointed his head in the direction of a tall, well-dressed woman walking towards them. The Abwehr was actively competing with Himmler's brutal Gestapo for the glory of trapping and killing off any, and all, opposition to the Nazi regime.

"Ingrid my darling! Good to see you!" Biggs said kissing the young woman on both cheeks.

Ingrid Schuyler was an attractive woman. She was six feet tall, with long blond hair which she had tied in a bun, light blue eyes, and a lean figure. She was built like a track athlete, which was fitting because she excelled in athletics as an undergraduate at Ludwig Maximillian University in Munich several years earlier. She was Bavarian and a patriot to the Fatherland. The spy had joined the Hitler youth in the late 1920s and eventually became a campus organiser when she entered university in the early 1930s. Her family had strong connections to the Nazi party which had been rewarded with contracts to manufacture components for Messerschmitt, the supplier of fighter aircraft to the Luftwaffe.

Schuyler was recruited by the local Abwehr directorate in Bavaria following her graduation from university. She had moved quickly up the intelligence ranks, her combination of good looks, a sharp intellect and ruthless demeanor giving her the perfect makeup for the spy business.

"What brings you to Lisbon, Nigel? I haven't seen you in ages!" she said gleefully, knowing Biggs was an SIS agent and had sprung him on the job, or so she correctly assumed.

Biggs lied unconvincingly for a seasoned spy, not that it mattered, as there was little he could do to cover his tracks. But he tried anyway. "We are a bit short-staffed darling, so I am helping on the trade desk for a few weeks. And what brings you to Lisbon, Ingrid?" Biggs asked the German trying to turn the tables on the Abwehr agent. "Last I heard you were at head office in Berlin."

"I have a roving mandate from our foreign office my dear," she replied smoothly.

"And let's face it, there is more business to be done in neutral ports like Lisbon." She continued with a knowing look pointed in the direction of Butler and Owens.

"And who are your friends?" she asked, smiling disingenuously at the Americans. Both looked uncomfortable as they stood for the formal introductions.

Biggs spoke up, trying to think up a plausible story on the fly.

"May I introduce Nash Owens and Dean Butler. They own a fishing business and are looking to expand in Europe," he said with the most conviction he could muster.

She shook hands with both. "And what kind of fishing are you interested in Mr. Owens?" Schuyler asked in leading fashion, suspecting the two had nothing to do with fishing or had ever put a line in the water. She thought to herself that Owens was probably a foreign service type, but she couldn't work out Butler. He looked a bit athletic and rough around the edges to be a diplomat. The fact they were Americans piqued her interest, and she wondered what they were up to with a MI-6 agent in tow. She would cable a report to Berlin later in the evening and organise for the men to be followed during their stay in Lisbon.

"Strictly commercial ma'am," Owens said, playing along and keeping explanations as brief as possible. "We have a fleet of fishing boats, and we need port and processing facilities in Europe. Lisbon seems to be a safe haven right now."

Still smiling and not at all interested in Owens' spin, Schuyler replied, "I am sure Nigel will look after you both. Now I must go, my dinner date has arrived." A well-to-do gentleman entered the hotel and waved discretely at the attractive spy. "Good to see you, Nigel. Don't be a stranger," she said in leading fashion, kissing him on the cheek and retiring from the bar to meet her date.

Butler spoke first, "Very nice. Too bad she is a Nazi spy."

Biggs nodded. "The worse kind. I am afraid the two of you have been sprung, as they say."

"Will she be trouble?" Owens asked looking worried.

"I am not sure, but Berlin will know about the two of you shortly, so your trip to the Congo may not be a surprise," Biggs said frowning. "I will see what we can do to get you out of Lisbon discretely. Assume you will be followed from now on."

Worried about their travel arrangements Owens asked Biggs, "The embassy is arranging our travel. Should we change flights?"

"No. But I will think up Plan B. Leave it to me."

"How did you run across her Biggs?" Butler inquired, wondering why in a business requiring discretion, the two knew each other, and more importantly what they did for their respective countries.

"Spy versus spy stuff Dean." Biggs started, withdrawing the pretence that he was anything other than a MI-6 agent.

"I was posted to the trade desk in Berlin a few years ago, and she was my contact at the German foreign ministry. She followed me around convinced that I was a spy. Ditto on my part." He continued. "We were both right as it turned out."

"It was all a bit tedious, but given we weren't as close to war with Germany as we are now, our standards, shall we say, were not that strict."

"She is very bright, and by reputation ruthless, so we need to beware of her." He said finishing the story.

"In the meantime, enjoy the sights of Lisbon accompanied by a German tour guide!" Biggs said cheekily, shrugging off the bad luck of the chance meeting with Schuyler. "I will be off gentlemen. Call the embassy if you need my help. I will let you know when I have worked out alternative travel arrangements." He finished his drink and left the hotel getting into the embassy's Jaguar which was parked in the hotel entrance.

"Well, that was a good start to our road trip." Butler concluded sarcastically to his travel companion.

"It certainly made things more interesting than they needed to be." Owens agreed.

"This is also not the ideal start to our relationship with Donovan," he continued, always cognizant of State Department politics.

"There's not a lot we can do about it partner." Butler replied philosophically, trying to cheer up his politically correct colleague.

'Drink up." Butler raised his glass, and the men finished their drinks and ordered another round.

* * *

Hofmayer, Meyer and Fischer set up camp in a small clearing in the jungle near the mine. The location allowed them to observe the comings-and-goings at the mine and work out how to take the uranium.

"I will look around captain and make sure there is no wildlife to interrupt our mission." Sergeant Fischer said carrying his rifle.

Meyer nodded. "Very good sergeant."

Hofmayer and Meyer began pitching the tent. Hofmayer asked his guide, "Who did you offend to get posted to this place captain?"

Smiling at the big German's attempt at humour, Meyer replied, "I volunteered. My family is originally from South Africa, and I grew up hunting. When the posting came up, I could not resist."

Hofmayer nodded respectfully, liking the fact that he was working with a 'yarpie'—a hardened, uncouth, and probably racist South African.

"Where is the railway captain?" he asked. The thick jungle made it difficult for him to find landmarks.

"Not far. You can see the rail spur at the mine," Meyer replied passing his binoculars to Hofmayer and pointing out the spur. "We will walk down. It is about a hundred metres from here."

Hofmayer asked, "Our best opportunity will be to take control of the train when it arrives to collect the uranium. Do you agree?"

"Yes. It makes sense that we should let the miners fill the box cars so we can reap the rewards," Meyer agreed. "But it will depend on how heavily defended the mine is."

"We can easily neutralize the guards and miners when it suits us," Hofmayer replied confidently.

"I am not at all concerned about a few blacks carrying guns." He continued revealing his racist side.

Fischer appeared from the bush. "The jungle is quiet captain. But sleep with your gun just in case."

Meyer agreed with his sergeant. "This is a dangerous country Herr Hofmayer. There are many ways to get killed if you are not careful."

Hofmayer tapped his rifle. "I am not concerned. Now let us find the railroad." The men picked up their weapons and strode into the jungle in search of the tracks.

Trudging their way through the dense undergrowth, it took them fifteen minutes to find the tracks. The jungle was quiet as the wildlife sat discretely hidden, watching, as the strangers invaded their paradise.

The railroad was a single track with narrow gauged rails. There were only a few feet of clear space on either side of the tracks as the jungle continually encroached on the railway. It was pruned only when the train made its way to the mine from Leopoldville and the engine cut through the invading vegetation.

"What do you think, Meyer?" Hofmayer asked.

"I think we should drive along the tracks to see if there is a good spot to ambush the train, in case it proves too difficult to take the mine," the captain replied.

"Yes. You are correct," Hofmayer agreed. "When we go back tomorrow, we will drive a distance along the tracks to see what we are up against."

The men walked a few hundred steps along the tracks in each direction, before giving up and trudging back through the jungle to their camp site.

* * *

The American destroyer USS Bangor was patrolling off the west coast of north Africa under orders from Admiral Knox. She had been on a training exercise with the Royal Navy and was in Gibraltar taking on provisions when she was ordered to find the Augustus.

She left the entrance of the Mediterranean and sailed southwest to the Canary Islands, turning west and cruised back and forth on a parallel course, hoping the Augustus would run across her.

Captain Dan Rogers was leaning on the handrail of the deck, outside the bridge, drinking coffee. He was joined by Executive Officer Tyler Jackson as they discussed the patrol route.

Rogers was pleased to get a real mission, as the constant training and routine patrols were boring for a naval officer itching to see action before he was too old to serve. His worse fear was that war would break out and he would end up in Norfolk sitting at a desk pushing paper. Jackson, on the other hand, was on his first tour having graduated the Naval Academy in Annapolis in 1938.

"No sign of her Tyler. She could not have got too far." Rogers said sounding frustrated.

Jackson agreed with the captain as he adjusted the heavy binoculars hanging from his neck, "She is an old freighter captain. She will not be making more than ten knots. We should have seen her by now."

"I think it's time to change location," Rogers decided. His instincts were telling him they were in the wrong position. "She is going to have to put into port to refuel before crossing the Atlantic and the Azores is the most likely spot. Let's move northwest Mr. Jackson. Hopefully, we will meet up with her south of the Azores."

"Aye captain." Jackson went to the bridge to issue the order.

The captains of the Bangor and U-073 had come to the same conclusion, putting them on a collision course in the mid Atlantic.

* * *

British Consul and SIS agent Peter Creighton was His Majesty's chief spy in the Belgian Congo. The embassy was small by British standards, housing only a handful of diplomats, so Creighton had to keep up his diplomatic pretence by also issuing the odd passport and visa to locals and ex-pats.

The son of a family doctor and a graduate of Cambridge, where he read classics, Creighton joined the Foreign Office in 1930. He was assigned to the African desk and after three years as a junior in the policy section, was posted to Tripoli as third secretary.

In 1935 he was recruited by the SIS to move into intelligence, which he decided was a much more exciting proposition than dealing with wayward ex-pats, tariffs and trade disputes. After two years working the desk at MI-6 in London he was posted to Leopoldville under cover as consul. The Congo until now had been a quiet backwater of inactivity and the uranium file was by far the most interesting piece of work to come his way since his arrival.

But he needed to know what was going on at the mine, and if there was German opposition in the country, so he invited the embassy's security chief, Lt. Colonel Dougal McInerney, to his office for a chat. It was time for his team to do some snooping.

McInerney was a Scot, in his early forties and a professional soldier. He oversaw a small detachment of twenty marines at the embassy. He was officious, by the book and a proud member of the Royal Scots Greys, or 2nd Dragoons, whose headquarters were the famous Edinburgh Castle. His distinguishing feature was a perfectly waxed handlebar mustache, and he proudly wore a kilt displaying the colours of his ancestors.

The son of farming gentry near Inverness, he was awarded a commission of lieutenant in the Great War, responsible for a platoon of regular infantry. McInerney managed to survive the Battles of Mons and Marne but was wounded at the Battle of Aisne in France, taking a machine gun shell in his left hip while leading his platoon over a trench. He was awarded the Distinguished Service Order for his leadership and gallantry in combat. He recovered and was encouraged to re-enlist after the war, where he became a career officer at the age of twenty-two.

McInerney's uncle Duncan served as a Conservative Member in the House of Lords and through that connection he secured a series of positions at embassies and high commissions in the British Empire. He was a single man with no family, so the embassy circuit suited him. However, he had to take the good with the bad, and the position in the Congo was a hardship posting, to use diplomatic vernacular.

McInerney knocked on the door of Creighton's office. Creighton was pouring a cup of tea. "Come in old boy," he said invitingly.

McInerney stood at attention. "Sir." McInerney announced formally.

"At ease old boy," Creighton commanded. McInerney stood at ease. "Cup of tea?" Creighton asked raising the tea pot as an invitation.

"Thank you, sir," He sat in a chair opposite Creighton's desk.

Creighton passed McInerney a cup of tea, his favored Prince of Wales blend. "The Foreign Office has a job for us Lt. Colonel," Creighton said evenly.

"Sir?" McInerney replied with a straight bat.

Creighton sipped his tea and briefed McInerney on the situation. "The Foreign Office thinks Jerry is up to no good down here. London thinks they are planning to pinch the uranium from the mine in Shinkolobwe. The Belgian company that owns the mine has given the uranium to the Americans, but the Yanks also think the Germans are going to try to steal it," he summarized providing McInerney with as much information as he had been given himself. "Can you look into it for me?"

McInerney nodded while sipping his tea. "Yes sir. I can send a couple of boys down to the mine to have a look around."

"I also need you to check the port and local hotels for any new faces from Germany. They think Jerry has dispatched agents to run the operation." Creighton continued. "There are only a handful of hotels in Leopoldville so it should not be too difficult a task. Also, get a couple of your boys to watch the German embassy. You never know, they could be hiding out there and we might get lucky."

"Yes sir. But if the Huns are not in Leopoldville, and are camping out somewhere, it will be like finding a proverbial needle in a haystack," McInerney said admitting that the task could prove difficult. "Anything else sir?"

"Yes, old boy. The Yanks are sending some of their people down here to get the uranium out of the country. I expect they will arrive in the next forty-eight hours," Creighton said. "It is their operation, but they will need our help. I will let you know when they arrive and what we can do to assist them. In the meantime, let us find out what Jerry is up to shall we?"

"Yes sir. I will make a full report as soon as we find out what is going on," McInerney replied.

"Very good Lt. Colonel. You are dismissed," Creighton said.

McInerney quickly finished his tea, stood at attention, clicked his heels together, saluted, and left the office. Creighton went back to his cup of tea. He picked up his pipe, tapped it on the side of his desk to clear any residue, filled it with tobacco, lit it, and took a drag, all the while wondering what the opposition was up to.

He agreed with McInerney's appraisal of the situation. They really were looking for a needle in a haystack. If the Germans had agents in the country, finding them would be difficult unless they were staying at the embassy, or in the relative comfort of a local hotel.

* * *

Bill Donovan checked into the Estoril hotel early the following morning and was stretched out on the bed, punch drunk with jet lag from the long journey. He was desperate for a bath, a decent meal, and several hours of uninterrupted sleep.

But first things first. He picked up the phone and called the operator. "Please connect me to Mr. Owens' room." The operator put him straight through.

Owens' phone rang and he picked it up. "Owens speaking."

Donovan got straight to the point. "It's Bill Donovan, Mr. Owens. Can you collect Mr. Butler and come to my room? I am next door in 814."

"Right away sir," Owens said with excitement in his voice. He immediately collected Butler and the two knocked on Donovan's door.

"Come in gentlemen," Donovan called to the men.

Owens greeted Donovan. "Good morning, sir."

Butler saluted and the men shook hands. Butler noted Donovan's frame was like his own, albeit Donovan was at least fifteen years older, in his early 40's. About six foot two inches and a fit 190 pounds, he also had large, rough hands, not what you would expect from a lawyer. Butler concluded Donovan could look after himself and suspected he had settled a number of legal disputes behind the courthouse rather than in front of the judge.

"Sit down gentlemen," Donovan said gesturing to the sofa. Both sat while Donovan took up position in an armchair.

"How was your flight sir?" Owens asked.

"Long," Donovan said in one word. He looked tired from the trip. His eyes had dark rings around them and were noticeably baggy. "What is the latest Mr. Owens?"

Owens filled in Donovan. "The Sangiers are in England and will be taking the Queen Mary to New York in the next few days, sir. The Brits are going to help us on the ground in the Belgian Congo."

"Good. And call me Bill. No formalities here." Donovan said.

"One more thing sir... uh, Bill," Butler said. "We were spotted last night by a German spy while we were meeting with our SIS contact. I gather all the spies around here know each other." He shook his head, still in disbelief that they had been sprung.

Frowning, but non-plussed, Donovan concluded pragmatically, "We'll need to assume that the Nazis know we are planning to take control of the uranium."

"Yes sir," Butler agreed. "In all likelihood, their agents in Brussels will be loose by now and have reported to Berlin that the Sangiers have left the country."

Donovan looked Butler in the eye. "You did not hurt them, I hope. I know I don't need to mention that we are not at war, nor do we want to start one."

"Just their pride sir," Butler replied with a cheeky smile, not feeling it necessary to mention the jaw of the agent he had broken.

"When are we flying to the Congo, Nash?" Donovan asked.

"The current itinerary has us going out tomorrow, Bill. We have a flight to Casablanca, but our SIS man is trying to find us alternative transport to throw the Germans off our tracks," Owens replied. "So, we may need to be ready at short notice. We are meeting our contact later in the morning to find out what he has planned."

Donovan yawned. "Ok men. I am going to get something to eat, take a bath and get some sleep. Let's have an early dinner tonight and finalize plans. You might as well spend the day enjoying the sights," Donovan said yawning again, cutting the young men loose for the day.

Owens and Butler let themselves out of his room.

Donovan picked up the phone and called room service. "Can I get a burger, fries, and a Coke?"

"Certainly, sir," the room service waiter said. "Give us fifteen minutes."

While he had been spoiled by Pan Am, he was a man of simple tastes and was pleased the hotel could accommodate him with a standard American meal.

* * *

Owens and Butler met Biggs two hours later at a café near the Lisbon market on the waterfront. The British spy had made alternative arrangements to get the Americans out of Portugal and wanted to share the details in a more discrete location, notwithstanding the unwelcome presence of a German agent following the Americans around for the day.

Biggs was sitting by himself reading a two-day old edition of the New York Herald-Tribune when the Americans arrived. His head was hidden by the newspaper. Owens and Butler sat down at the table next to the spy and ordered coffee, ignoring their MI-6 contact. For all intents and purposes, it looked as if the men were strangers who happened to be at the same café. Owens was carrying a tourist guide and pretended to be reading the book.

"Any news Biggs?" Owens asked while he read up on the Lisbon market. Always the nervous one, getting sprung by the Abwehr agent had led to a sleepless night for the young diplomat.

"We have a plan to get you out tonight without Jerry being any the wiser as to your destination," Biggs said speaking behind the cover of his newspaper.

"What have you got in mind?" Butler asked, also ignoring Biggs while pretending to be speaking to his American travel companion.

"The Royal Air Force runs a routine supply flight to Gibraltar," Biggs explained from behind the daily. "They refuel at the air force base here. The three of you can catch a ride to Gibraltar and then the RAF will fly you to Casablanca. You can get a commercial flight into Leopoldville from there."

"Sounds easy enough," Butler said. "But how do we lose our tails? There is a car sitting outside the hotel and our friend Fritz is hiding in the shop doorway down the street. The Nazis are not a subtle lot." A rotund German male was pretending to be interested in ladies' shoes and handbags, looking in a shop window a few doors up the street from the cafe.

"Leave that to me old man," Biggs said as he turned the page of the newspaper. "We will get you a head start, and once Jerry figures out that we have given them the slip, they will go looking for the three of you at Lisbon Airport. The Air Force base is on the other side of the city. They will have no idea you are flying RAF. Check out at 7 p.m. tonight. An embassy car will pick you up in the hotel driveway."

Parker-Biggs finished his coffee, put on his hat and sunglasses, and folded his newspaper, putting it under his arm. "Must go! See you this evening," he said without looking at the Americans. He paid his tab and left the table, walking in the opposite direction of the German tail, and towards the centre of Lisbon. The German stayed where he was, waiting for the two Americans to move on.

"Doesn't sound like much of a plan to me," Butler said complaining to Owens.

Owens was more confident in his smooth-talking colleague and relieved that he had found them alternative transportation. "I cannot wait to see what he has in mind. Let's see the sights shall we." He turned his head to look at the German who was still evaluating the latest women's fashion trends. "Fritz looks like he could use some exercise." They paid their tab, got up, and left the café, walking at a steady clip which forced the visibly unfit German agent to follow them at a trot.

Owens and Butler looked at each other and cracked smiles, knowing they were both younger and fitter, and had every intention of spending the afternoon making their tail's life a misery.

* * *

Donovan enjoyed his burger notwithstanding the odd flavor of the tomato sauce. They did not have American ketchup in Portugal and the local brew had a strange mix of spices.

After taking a long bath he went to bed and was comatose until a wake-up call roused him at 5 p.m. He took a shower to shake off the rust, got dressed, and went to the front desk to send a telegram to his wife letting her know that he had arrived in Lisbon safely.

He then met up with Owens and Butler, and the three Americans had an early dinner in the hotel's plush, silver service dining room.

"Eat up gentlemen," Donovan said motioning to the young diplomats' beautifully presented meals. Their entrees were served on Royal Doulton bone china dinner plates, delivered under sterling silver bowl shaped covers by a white gloved waiter. "This will be the last decent meal we get for a while if the food in the Congo is anything like the fare in Ethiopia," Donovan said, reflecting on his recent travels to East Africa.

Butler and Owens picked up their silver flatware and began devouring their entrees. Fillets of grilled sea bass, with lemon butter and dill, served with potatoes dauphinoise and fresh vegetables. Donovan ordered a club sandwich, deep fried onion rings and a Coke, again pleasantly surprised that the plush hotel would cater to his basic tastes. He left the ketchup alone this time around.

"What were you doing in Ethiopia, Bill?" Owens asked.

"The President wanted me to find out what the Italians were up to," Donovan said without providing much detail. "As the two of you have probably figured out the government doesn't have a service like the SIS to keep an eye on our enemies, or our friends. So, the President asked me to check things out. As it turns out Mussolini was a very generous host. I expect he would ditch Hitler in a second if a better offer came along."

"That said, as fascist dictators go, he is definitely bringing up the rear. Hitler and Stalin leave him for dead as far as thugs go. Franco as well." He continued, concluding his abbreviated assessment of the Italian dictator, better known as Il Duce.

"Did the Germans have someone following you around all day?" Donovan asked the men, keen to change the subject.

Owens and Butler shared a brief laugh while Butler explained their day of sightseeing. "Yeah, but he gave up after a couple of hours. We set a quick pace along the waterfront and the poor bastard had to run to keep up."

"He was waiting for us at the hotel when we returned."

Donovan smiled at the thought of the younger men making life difficult for the German. He also decided they would be up to the task of repatriating the uranium, a doubt that had been nagging him since he had taken on the assignment. Their combination of intellect and a willingness to do whatever was necessary to get the job done impressed him.

Butler got back to business in between bites. "Parker-Biggs has arranged to get us on a Royal Air Force supply flight to Gibraltar, Bill. They re-fuel here before heading south."

Owens always mindful of their travel itinerary checked his watch, "He has a diversion planned so we need to be ready for 7 p.m. About an hour from now."

"The Nazis are probably expecting us out on the Sabena flight in the morning—the original flight we were booked on. We still have tickets for that flight in case they check with the airline. Once we get to Gibraltar the RAF is going to fly us to Casablanca and we will pick up a flight from there into Leopoldville."

Donovan nodded as he munched on an onion ring. "Sounds good. I expect we are going to need heavy armor when we get there. Have you arranged that Nash?"

"We have the Brits' garrison at our disposal Bill," Owens said. "They should be able to supply everything we need."

Donovan nodded again, mentally knocking another item off his to-do list. "When we get there, I want to meet up with the Brits to get the lay of the land," he added.

"Parker-Biggs has everything organized," Owens replied. "Someone from the embassy will meet us at the airport."

Donovan looked at his watch, which was showing 6:17p.m. He put cash on the table to cover the bill. "Let's get moving gentlemen. Meet me downstairs in a half hour." They got up and went back to their rooms to pack.

Meantime, Nigel Parker-Biggs was outside the hotel waiting for the Americans. He was speaking to the doorman and pulled a stack of Portuguese escudo out of his pocket. He handed it to the cheerful, middle-aged man, who readily agreed to help with the task at hand, laughing at the thought of the forthcoming mischief at the Germans' expense, as well as the remuneration for orchestrating the practical joke.

Donovan, Owens and Butler checked out and followed the porter, who had their bags on a trolley, to the curb. A black Mercedes was parked in the drive at the far curb in front of the hotel. Two leather-coated German-types were sitting in the front seat watching the Americans. The driver started the car and prepared to follow the men when they left the hotel.

The doorman whistled and signaled two cabs to pull up. He passed money to the first taxi driver who moved forward and parked directly behind the Mercedes pretending to wait for a passenger.

The doorman then leaned in the window of the second cab and passed money to the driver, who immediately pulled directly in front of the Mercedes, blocking his exit. Sensing something was up, the German driver tried to reverse and then go forward to give himself space to pull out. Unfortunately for the Nazi, the taxis had him blocked in.

Finally, a dark green Jaguar with diplomatic plates drove into the hotel entrance to pick up the Donovan party. Parker-Biggs tipped his hat at the Americans as they got into the Jag.

"I hope you had a pleasant stay gentlemen," the doorman said with a smile. Donovan gave the doorman and porter generous tips as they got into the embassy car and departed the hotel. The entire operation took less than two minutes.

The driver of the Mercedes got out of his car as the Americans departed and started abusing the taxi drivers. "Get out of the fucking way you fucking imbeciles!" He ranted in a thick German accent.

The taxi drivers ignored him, getting out of their vehicles, and lighting up cigarettes. Several other drivers who were waiting for fares got out of their cars and joined the two drivers. The Germans were totally outnumbered and forced to back off. There was no love lost between the Portuguese and Germans. The driver and his passenger ran to the end of the driveway and threw their arms in the air knowing they had been pranked by one of the oldest tricks in the spy manual. Parker-Biggs disappeared into the hotel and joined one of his colleagues at the bar for a well-deserved drink.

CHAPTER FIVE

THE GERMANS PLOT

Hofmayer, Meyer and Fischer were watching the entrance to the mine, which to that point had been quiet. Aside from a couple of locals looking for work, nobody else had visited the mine that day. The mine also had little security, giving Hofmayer even more confidence that taking the uranium would be straight forward. There was only one guard at the main gate and Hofmayer amused himself by taking aim with his hunting rifle and grunting, "Bang, you are dead," faking a shot for his own twisted entertainment.

Early in the afternoon, a Bedford MWD lorry pulled up to the main gate and two British soldiers got out. They were directed to the office by the guard. "We have company captain," Hofmayer said to Meyer as he watched the soldiers drive up to the office. They were greeted at the door of the office by a middle-aged white man.

"I take it the man at the office door is manager of the mine." Hofmayer mused, as he continued to evaluate how much of a threat the miners would be if the Germans tried to take control of the mine.

"It looks that way," Meyer said agreeing with the spy. "There is no one else that I can see who looks to be in charge."

"It also looks as if your visit here is perhaps not so secret after all," Meyer thought out loud, wondering why British soldiers would come all this way for any reason other than having been ordered to check on security.

"Perhaps," Hofmayer conceded. "But it is a long way back to Leopoldville and the road is very dangerous."

Sensing the game, Meyer encouraged Hofmayer's thinking. "Accidents are very common Herr Hofmayer."

Cracking an evil smile, Hofmayer egged Meyer on. "What do you suggest captain? Big game hunting?"

"I think an accident Herr Hofmayer," the captain said with an equally devious grin. "There is a bend in the road by the river. If you do not navigate the curve you will end up in the river. And the crocodiles are very hungry at this time of year."

"Very good Meyer. Let's be on our way. I am sure the soldiers will not be too long."

"Let's be off Fischer," Meyer ordered. "Do you know the curve?"

"Yes. I know the one," Fischer confirmed dutifully. "It is about ten kilometres up the road. We will find an ambush site close by." The Germans jumped into their Kübelwagen and drove back through the thick undergrowth to the main road.

* * *

In the middle of the Atlantic, south of the Azores, the captain of the Augustus was standing on the foredeck next to the bridge, working his binoculars over the empty ocean to his north. The weather was calm and warm and had thus far cooperated during the voyage. A young deckhand came running towards him from the stern deck, waving his binoculars and pointing, "Captain! A submarine south of us," the panicky deckhand cried, fearful the submarine was German.

Van Hoeven turned around and scanned the ocean south of their position, very quickly spotting the sub. "She is several kilometres away, but I cannot make her out." He said to the sailor.

"Take no chances. Engines to full speed." He ordered, putting his head inside the bridge door and issuing the instruction to the helmsman. "Let us see if we can beat whoever she is to the Azores. The islands belong to Portugal and are neutral. If the sub is German, which I suspect given the lack of radio contact, they will not dare to board us on Portuguese soil."

The Augustus' aging engines kicked into full gear and the cargo ship struggled to ten knots. While slower than the sub, which could run almost twenty knots on the surface, it would take some time for the freighter to be run down by the submarine.

Van Hoeven was playing for time and hoping for a miracle.

The U-Boat was about ten kilometres south of the freighter and slowly gaining ground. It would take her a few hours to catch the freighter and thus far the captain was being patient knowing that time was on his side. Captain Jaanzen and Executive Officer Schneider were on deck keeping an eye on the Augustus when a sailor climbed onto the conning tower platform. "Captain. We have another sonar contact. About fifteen kilometres east-northeast of our position," the sailor reported.

Looking northeast through his binoculars Jaanzen saw smoke billowing from a double-stacked ship well in the distance. "She looks like a destroyer Schneider. Either British or American probably. I doubt the Italians would have a ship this far west so we must assume she is not an ally." He passed the binoculars to Schneider for confirmation.

"She is in a hurry whoever she is," he continued. The dark smoke belching out of her stacks was a giveaway that the destroyer was moving at speed.

Looking through the binoculars Schneider nodded. "I agree captain. What are your orders?"

Jaanzen said with determination, "Full ahead! Let's run down the freighter and take her. Get a boarding party ready. We will change flags before our competitor is any the wiser. Signal Canaris and let him know our plan and that either the Americans or the British are also pursuing the target."

Schneider slid down the ladder to the bridge to relay the orders and get the men ready for the forthcoming action.

Back on the Augustus a lookout also spotted the American destroyer and immediately reported the sighting to Van Hoeven. The captain turned around and saw the smoke plumes belching from the stacks of the large vessel.

"She looks to be ten to twelve kilometres east of us," the lookout said.

"Can you make her out sailor?" Van Hoeven replied squinting at the ship in the distance.

Shaking his head the lookout replied, "No, but she is intent on catching us. She must be making at least thirty knots."

The cat-and-mouse game had suddenly become more interesting, Van Hoeven made his decision and pointed in the direction of the Bangor. "Change course and head for that ship!" he yelled as the excitement brewed. "I am betting the sub is German, so we have nothing to lose now. As much speed as you can get out of this old sow mister!"

* * *

On the Bangor, the captain was back on the bridge, drinking a mug of coffee, as the executive officer came in to report that spotters had identified two ships west and southwest of the destroyer.

"One ship is about ten kilometres west of us and the other about ten kilometres south of the first, sir," Jackson reported.

"Can you make out what, or who, they are Tyler?" Rogers asked.

"Not yet sir," Jackson replied. "Although the more southerly contact doesn't have a stack so could be a sub."

Rogers put down his mug and issued an order to the helmsman. "Ok. Let's catch up and find out who is who. Full ahead mister." The ship, which had already been travelling near maximum speed, picked up a few more knots and was soon gliding through the calm sea at better than thirty knots.

"Let's get between the two ships Mr. Jackson," Rogers ordered. "If one of the ships is the Augustus you can bet the second one is a German trying to catch her up."

"Aye, captain," Jackson affirmed.

"And sound general quarters Mr. Jackson," Rogers ordered, raising his voice and thumping his fist on his chair as the adrenalin rush kicked in. "I don't want to be caught with our pants down. Message fleet. Tell them the situation and request orders."

"If one of the ships is German, can we fire on it?" Jackson asked, seeking clarification of the rules of engagement.

Rogers shook his head. "Not directly, unless fleet changes our orders, or we are fired upon." Then he said with a devious smile, "but we can be a nuisance." One way or the other he would make sure the German vessel did not get her prey, if as he suspected the trailing vessel was from the Kriegsmarine. Rogers did not know what the cargo was, that was so important to both Germany and the United States, but when Knox was calling the shots, he knew he had leeway to take some chances.

Five minutes later the radio operator walked the short distance from the radio room to the bridge. He gave a message to the executive officer who passed it to the captain.

"Orders sir," Jackson announced with anticipation.

The captain looked at the message and read it to the crew. "Men. Fleet says to use all possible means to prevent the Augustus being boarded, but not to sink the trailing ship if it is German."

A lookout entered the bridge to confirm, as the captain suspected, that the ship was a German submarine, and it was chasing a freighter with a Belgian flag. Rogers sipped his coffee, then nodded his understanding and issued instructions to the crew.

"Once we get into firing range put one across the sub's bow. They need to think we are serious," the captain ordered trying to work out how far he could go before getting in trouble with Knox. "If the sub does not cease and desist, we will keep firing on her until she does. We need to keep her away from the freighter."

Rogers turned to Jackson. "Tyler, I am interpreting the order to mean we can hurt the sub, just not sink her. Do you agree?"

Jackson re-read the order and nodded his agreement. "She can survive the odd dent captain," he said, covering his captain's ass just in case. Both officers would need to file a report following the engagement and it was important, for both their careers, that their interpretation of the order was the same.

To emphasize the importance of their mission, Rogers revealed to his crew that the orders came directly from Knox. Looking at the sailors on the bridge he was pleased at what he saw. By the look in the eyes of the young crew, his men were focused on the task at hand. They were ready to do whatever they needed to do to make sure the Augustus would not be taken by the Germans.

The USS Bangor was ready for action. War or no war.

* * *

On the Augustus, Captain Van Hoeven was keeping a close eye on the U-Boat wondering what she would do now that the freighter had made a starboard turn and was cruising at full speed towards the destroyer. He did not have to wait long to find out as a shell exploded a hundred metres off her bow.

"Begin evasive manoeuvres. Zigzag sailor," Van Hoeven coolly ordered his helmsman. The captain was not the panicky type, and being a stubborn Dutchman, he was also not going to give up without a fight.

"Keep us moving in the direction of that destroyer," he re-affirmed, making sure the helmsman understood his order. Water erupted fifty metres off the bow of the Augustus. The Germans were finding their mark.

The captain did not think the sub wanted to sink the Augustus or she would have torpedoed her by now. But he did not know what the sub would do now that an 'enemy' destroyer was on station.

As Van Hoeven was thinking about his next course of action, the Bangor was about to get into the fray. The destroyer was close enough to engage the submarine and the Bangor's gunnery crews were lining her up.

Van Hoeven and his crew watched the drama unfold as the Bangor fired its 125mm cannon. A shell landed off the sub's port side, hitting the ocean about forty metres away. This was followed by a second shell that exploded closer and sent seawater gushing onto the sub's deck.

"It looks as if you made the right bet captain," the Augustus' executive officer said now that it was clear that the destroyer was friendly.

"It appears so," the captain replied evenly, not yet willing to admit that they were out of danger.

As if to confirm his fears, the sub fired two more shells at the Augustus, both landing just off her bow. But the destroyer was getting more aggressive, and a shell barely missed the U-Boat, sending up a geyser next to her. The game of chicken would be decided in the next few minutes.

"That was close," Van Hoeven remarked to his executive officer as if he were commentating on a sporting event. "I expect the next one will sink her," he added hopefully.

As if Van Hoeven had read the mind of the U-Boat's captain, the crew on the sub started to evacuate the deck with the dive alarm sounding a few seconds later.

"She is going under," the clearly relieved captain said to his executive officer.

The executive officer took a deep breath then slowly exhaled, sharing the captain's sense of relief that they might yet live to fight another day.

* * *

On the bridge of the Bangor the executive officer and captain watched the German sub withdraw from the fight. "We got her attention Mr. Jackson," Captain Rogers said as he watched the sub begin to dive. "She ceased fire and is submerging. Stay at battle stations. We will depth charge her if she does not keep her distance."

Nodding, Jackson acknowledged the order. "Yes, captain."

"And keep an eye on the sonar Mr. Jackson. I do not want to be blindsided. Signal the Augustus and tell her to close up and we will escort her into port. Message fleet," Rogers ordered. "Tell Knox that we have caught up with the Augustus and the enemy has retired. Tell him we are heading for the Azores to refuel and take on provisions. We should be in port tomorrow or early the next day. Also, find out the whereabouts of the second escort, and request that she meet us in the Azores."

"Yessir!" Jackson said enthusiastically, knowing the Bangor had saved the day. The Augustus was out of trouble and now safely on its way to neutral Portuguese territory in the company of the United States Navy.

* * *

Hofmayer, Meyer, and Fischer were waiting for the British troops to return from the mine. They had set up an ambush site in the jungle across the road from the river. The road curved sharply at that point and was less than three metres from the crocodile-infested river.

"We have an unobstructed view of the road from here captain," Fischer said as the camouflaged group dug in.

"And a good line of fire," Captain Meyer observed as he worked to get his scope centred on the ambush site.

Hofmayer was also pleased. "A perfect location and a lot of crocodiles in the river and on the banks." He focused his scope on a crocodile sunning itself on the riverbank. "Now we wait."

* * *

The flight carrying Donovan, Owens and Butler landed without incident at Leopoldville airport and they disembarked the twin engine DC3, standing on the tarmac to get their bearings. A local airline employee pointed them in the direction of the rudimentary arrivals hut.

"I take it the military-type over there is our ride," Donovan said pointing his head in the direction of a soldier in British military garb who was standing behind the fence looking at the men.

"I expect so. I will ask," Owens replied. He walked over to the terminal to meet the officer.

Butler looked up at the intense sun, which combined with the heat and humidity, was quite a shock from the Mediterranean climate from which they had just come. "Hot enough for you Bill?"

Donovan agreed. "Ethiopia was pretty unforgiving. This is right up there."

Owens waved at Donovan and Butler to join him. They walked over to the fence near the arrivals building. "May I introduce Lt. Colonel McInerney. He is head of security at the British embassy and has been keeping an eye out for our German friends," Owens said, making the formal introductions. Butler saluted McInerney and the officer returned the salute as they exchanged military courtesies.

"Welcome to Leopoldville gentlemen," the Scot said with his thick accent. "I will take you to your hotel and update you on our activities." They had their passports stamped, collected their luggage, walked to the embassy car, and drove off.

"What is the latest McInerney?" Donovan asked as the 1938 Jaguar Saloon navigated the streets of Leopoldville occasionally avoiding pedestrians who appeared not to understand, or care about, the rules of the road.

McInerney updated the Americans. "My boys have been keeping an eye on the German embassy as well as checking the local hotels and the port. I sent two men to the mine. They should be back tonight sometime."

"Anything interesting?" Donovan asked.

"Not much. A few German businessmen arrived recently. One is worth a look, if for no other reason than he likes the local ladies and fits the stereotype of an arrogant Hun. He was picked up yesterday morning at his hotel, by a couple of hunters and has not returned, according to the doorman. The doorman said the truck was loaded with supplies. So, he could be our man, or a legitimate hunter out for game.

The port manager at Matadi told me a diplomat from the German embassy was asking questions about shipping leaving the port. Once the boys get back from the mine, I will let you know what is going on down there," McInerney continued.

"So, if the Nazis have spies in country, they are keeping a low profile," Butler concluded.

"It certainly looks that way," McInerney replied. "That said, they are certainly keeping an eye on things, if the port manager is to be believed. It also would not surprise me if the hunting party turned out to be the spy ring we are looking for. But I have no evidence for the moment. The German embassy is also quiet. Just routine traffic in and out."

"This uranium sounds like a hot potato sirs. If the Huns have people on the ground, they could be hiding in the jungle, and we would never see them," McInerney cautioned.

They pulled into the driveway of the Sabena Hotel and Guest House. "Leopoldville's finest gentlemen," McInerney announced with a grin. "By that I mean the rooms are air conditioned, the windows are barred, and the beer is cold. Our man here, Creighton, will pop around for dinner tonight if that suits. Say eight o'clock?"

Donovan nodded. "Eight is perfect. We are going to need to outfit ourselves Lt. Colonel. Can you help us?"

"The embassy is at your disposal sir," McInerney confirmed. "We should have everything you need. Come by in the morning and we will get you kitted."

"Good. We will see you tomorrow then," Donovan replied.

* * *

The Germans had been biding their time waiting in the jungle across the road from the river. It was starting to get dark, and the men were getting restless waiting for their prey.

The British soldiers finally made their appearance just before sunset. They were cruising along in their truck at a leisurely forty kilometres per hour.

"Vehicle approaching Hofmayer," Fischer reported spying the vehicle through his binoculars. "The truck we have been waiting for, I think. There are two soldiers in it."

Hofmayer turned to Meyer, confirming the plan of attack. "So, we will shoot the tires Meyer?"

Meyer nodded. "You take the front, and I will take the rear. Wait until just before they reach the curve. When the tires are blown, they will lose control and the truck will roll into the river."

"Fischer, you are second shot if either of us miss," Meyer said to his sergeant.

"Yes captain," Fischer acknowledged.

"I won't miss," Hofmayer grunted with his usual arrogant confidence.

The truck approached the bend. "On my signal," Meyer commanded. A few seconds later the truck came into view and the captain called out, "Now!"

Both men fired. They hit their targets, blowing out the truck's tires. The vehicle careened out of control and rolled over. As it rolled down the bank the soldiers were thrown into the river and then trapped beneath the semi-submerged vehicle, which landed on top of the poor men.

Sensing a good meal, a half-dozen crocodiles scurried off the bank and attacked the helpless soldiers who screamed in both terror and pain. Their death was quick. The hungry predators took the soldiers apart as if they had not eaten in months.

"Excellent shooting captain," Hofmayer laughed, enjoying the schadenfreude. "Two less Brits to kill when our Führer invades Europe."

"Thank you, Hofmayer," Meyer said, also enjoying the bloody spectacle. "Likewise, your marksmanship was outstanding."

"Very good," chortled the pathological Hofmayer, now in a jovial mood. "Tomorrow, I want to find a place to take the train. The mine poses no threat if they are not expecting us."

"And even if they are, they won't stop us." He continued, the bloodlust running through his veins.

"Agreed," Meyer said. "Fischer, let's get back to camp and tomorrow we will find a site to take care of the train."

Taking camouflage off the Volkswagen, Fischer said dutifully, "Yes, captain. When you are ready." While his superiors had enjoyed the murderous blood sport, the young sergeant took no pleasure in witnessing the murder of the British soldiers.

* * *

SIS agent Peter Creighton arrived at the Sabena hotel promptly at 8 p.m. He joined Donovan, Owens and Butler at the hotel bar, which was next to the outdoor dining room and set in a beautifully manicured garden, at the rear of the property.

The garden featured a colourful mix of local and imported shrubs. Local species included orchids, black guarea and wooden pears. They blended nicely with the azaleas and rhododendrons that had been imported into the country by well meaning colonialists.

The groundskeeper kept the lawn perfectly manicured giving the local gentry a civilized venue for a game of croquet, followed by a gin and tonic or strong Belgian ale. The landscaping also provided hotel guests with a visual respite from the drabness and poverty of the street frontage, less than a hundred metres away.

"Good evening gentlemen, my name is Peter Creighton. I am consul at the British embassy." The MI-6 agent announced using his cover, rather pointlessly, as he introduced himself to the American contingent. "I hope the quarters we have arranged are satisfactory."

He shook hands with the Americans and sat down to join the discussion. Donovan did the introductions. "The rooms are fine, thanks Mr. Creighton. My name is Bill Donovan. Call me Bill. My colleagues, Nash Owens and Lieutenant Commander Dean Butler," Donovan said, introducing the American team and pointing out each in turn. "My two colleagues are assigned to the American embassy in Brussels and helped the mine owner and his family escape the Nazis."

"Very good." Creighton said acknowledging the achievements of the young diplomats.

"Please call me Peter. I have two dispatches for you Bill," Creighton said toning down the formalities. He handed the messages to Donovan.

The waiter approached the table. "May I get you a refreshment sir?"

"Gin and tonic please old man. The Botanist if you have it. A slice of lemon and one ice cube," Creighton replied specifying his desired mixology. The waiter confirmed the bar had his favored gin and left to prepare the cocktail.

"What's the latest Bill?" Butler asked Donovan.

Reading the messages Donovan updated the table. "The Navy caught up with the freighter south of the Azores. They are going to refuel in the Azores and sail for New York as soon as the second escort arrives. The Germans came within a whisker of taking her. They had a sub chasing the freighter. A couple of shots across her bow by one of our destroyers curbed her enthusiasm."

Looking up at his colleagues at the table, he cautioned the group. "I think we can safely assume the Germans are not going to give up without a fight."

Butler wanted to know what firepower could be brought to bear on the Nazis if there was a fight. "How many soldiers do you have at the embassy Mr. Creighton, and what types of weapons do you have in the arsenal?"

"We have a detachment of twenty marines Lieutenant Commander," Creighton said. "You met McInerney today. He commands the detachment. Captain Henderson is his deputy. The arsenal comprises mainly small weapons. Handguns, Enfield's, two Vickers and a handful of Brens plus grenades and fifty kilos of 808 explosives and fuses. McInerney will show you the kit in the morning."

Creighton added, "The marines' mission is purely defensive. Our troops ensure the embassy is secure. Most of the boys are green. Except for McInerney and Henderson none of them have any experience on the battlefield. The Belgians run the country with an iron fist and security issues are minimal, so our boys spend their days training when they are not on guard duty. A bit of action will do them good," he said to reinforce the message that while small, the garrison would also be more than capable of dealing with German agents if there was a fight.

Donovan waited for Creighton to finish before reading the second message. "The freighter for the second load will be here in the next seventy-two hours. She is being escorted by a destroyer. The ships left the Canaries three days ago and are currently sailing down the west coast."

Owens jumped into the discussion as he thought through the logistics of the task. "We better get to the mine and start loading the ore. How do they get it from the mine to the port, Mr. Creighton?"

"By train Mr. Owens," Creighton said. "The engine is at the Leopoldville rail yard and will go to the mine when they are ready to ship the load. The journey is about 250 kilometres. The rail cars are at the mine, so the train just needs to hitch up and be on its way."

"How long does it take to load Mr. Creighton... Peter?" Owens asked.

"I don't know much about the logistics Nash," Creighton conceded. "You will need to discuss that with the local manager. His name is De Suter, and he is based at the mine."

The waiter arrived with a gin and tonic. "Thanks, old man," Creighton acknowledged cordially to the young black waiter as he smelled the telltale aroma of the fine Scottish gin.

"Can you provide us with a vehicle Mr. Creighton?" Donovan asked. "We will work independently and be in touch when we need your help."

"Of course. We can arrange that in the morning. What else do you need from me?" The MI-6 man asked.

Donovan continued, "McInerney said there was a suspicious German who checked into a local hotel earlier in the week. Can one of your people keep an eye on him and let me know what he is up to? Also get a picture of him if you can."

"With pleasure," Creighton replied in proper British colonial-speak.

"Finally, can you find out if there are any ships due into port in the next few days. If the Germans are serious, they will have despatched a freighter to carry the ore," Donovan said.

"Of course. What will the three of you be up to?" Creighton enquired.

"First order of business is the mine," Donovan said. "I want to meet the manager and see how we can get the uranium to the port without the Germans interfering with it. I also want to get the train down to the mine. Even if it must sit there for a couple of days."

"Good thinking Mr. Donovan," Creighton said. "Best to have all the assets in one place. We can send troops to help with security if you think it would be warranted."

"We'll let you know when we get back from the mine," Donovan responded with a furrowed brow knowing his team did not have home field advantage on this mission and were guessing what, if anything, the Germans were up to.

The waiter returned. "Dinner is served sirs. Please follow me." The group got up and were escorted to their table.

*　*　*

In the Atlantic, U-073, having retreated from the American destroyer, circled back southeast and was now patrolling off the west African coast near southern Mauritania. She was running on the surface to recharge her batteries and await orders.

Jaanzen was on deck enjoying the moonlit evening. A cool easterly breeze blowing off the Atlantic towards the African continent kept the temperature a very pleasant twenty-five degrees.

Executive Officer Frits Schneider climbed up the ladder from the bridge, hopping onto the conning tower platform. Both men's demeanors were starting to improve as they recovered from the near-death experience of being attacked by an American destroyer.

Schneider handed an eyes-only message to Jaanzen who took a quick look at its source. Seeing it was from Großadmiral Donitz, head of the German Navy, he opened it straight away.

"What does it say captain?" Schneider asked, barely able to contain his excitement at the thought of the head of the navy issuing orders to the sub.

Pursing his lips and furrowing his brow, as he took in their next assignment, Jaanzen ordered. "We need to head due south Frits. Ahead full. Stay on the surface!"

"Where to captain?" Schneider could not resist wanting in on the secret.

"Eyes only. Sorry Frits," Jaanzen said sympathetically. "I will tell you when we get closer to our assigned location."

CHAPTER SIX

RATTLING THE CAGES

B ack in Washington, German Chargé Affaires, Hans Thomsen, arrived at the State Department to complain about an alleged incident between a German submarine and an American destroyer.

German and American diplomatic relations were testy at best. The year before, in 1938, the United States withdrew its ambassador to protest the Nazi's Kristallnacht policy, which was designed by Nazi Germany to incite thuggery against Jewish people, their businesses, and places of worship. In retaliation, Germany did likewise, leaving Thomsen the senior diplomat in the United States.

"Mr. Hull will see you now Mr. Thomsen. Please follow me." Hull's secretary gestured to the German diplomat.

"Thank you madame," he said formally, and followed the middle-aged woman to the Secretary of State's meeting room.

He was seated when Hull came into the room and took his place on the opposite side of the meeting table. "Good afternoon, Mr. Thomsen," Hull said cordially, knowing he was about to take a diplomatic serve from the Nazi.

"It is good to see you again Herr Secretary," the Chargé Affaires said in a business-like fashion.

"I take it this isn't a social call," Hull said evenly. "Have we done something to raise the ire of the German republic, Herr Thomsen?"

Thomsen got straight to the point. "We have a report that one of your destroyers fired on one of our submarines. If true, the Reich would regard this incident as an act of war." In diplomatic speak this was about as strong a rebuke that could be issued by one country to another. Hull could tell the Americans were getting under Hitler's skin given Thomsen's stern demeanor and direct language.

Pleading ignorance, Hull feigned concern for the welfare of the German submariners. "If true Mr. Thomsen, I hope no one was hurt."

"Thankfully not. And the incident was not a figment of our navy's imagination," Thomsen replied forcefully.

Hull took that to mean Thomsen had evidence of the attack. "You understand, Mr. Thomsen, that I will need to contact the Secretary of the Navy and get a full report."

"Please do," Thomsen replied. "My Führer is in no mood to tolerate America interfering in the Reich's affairs."

"I can assure you, Mr. Thomsen, that the United States government has no interest interfering in European matters," Hull said communicating the standard American foreign policy line. "However, for matters of international law, it is the United States' position to protect its interests and also, where appropriate, act in self defence." Diplomatic speak for telling the Germans to back off the uranium, or else.

"Very well, Herr Hull," Thomsen replied playing along. "The next time there is a 'legal argument' I suggest it is referred to a court to be resolved in a civilized manner."

"A very good suggestion Mr. Thomsen," Hull said tongue-in-cheek, trying not to laugh at the hypocrisy coming from the mouth of his German counterpart. "Please excuse me. I have another matter to deal with. My secretary will show you out." Hull said, rising curtly and leaving the meeting room, diplomatic speak for don't waste my time.

Hull's secretary immediately appeared in the room with two burly marines in tow and Thomsen was shown the door.

* * *

Early the next morning Donovan, Owens, and Butler arrived at the British embassy to collect vehicles and weapons. Creighton and McInerney were waiting to meet the Americans and provide whatever assistance the men needed. The embassy receptionist made the obligatory offer of a cup of tea, which was politely declined by the coffee-loving Americans.

Creighton greeted Donovan's team. "Good morning gentlemen. I hope your rooms were comfortable and you slept well."

"Everything was fine thanks Mr. Creighton," Donovan replied. "We have been discussing our priorities and have decided to split up for the day. Owens and Butler are going to the mine, and I will check the port, so you don't need to send any of your staff to Matadi."

"Very good," Creighton replied. "Now what can we offer you from His Majesty's arsenal?"

"We are going to need trucks and weapons Mr. Creighton. A couple of rifles just in case. Also, sidearms," Butler started.

"I can give you a hand with that," McInerney confirmed.

Owens admitted sheepishly, "I have never fired a gun, Lieutenant Colonel. Do you have something for a beginner?" His honest admission was met with laughter.

"A Bren light machine gun will do the trick Mr. Owens," McInerney said. "Tidy weapon for a beginner. Just point and spray the Huns or anything else that gets in your way. It comes with a tripod so is nice and stable if you are in a prone position."

"Remember to flip the safety switch before you pull the trigger."

McInerney turned to Butler. "And you sir. Any preferences?"

"I brought my shotgun but could use a rifle and sidearm if you can spare two weapons," he said, proudly showing off his custom-made Griffin & Howe. "Also, some grenades just in case."

"We can accommodate you," McInerney nodded.

"Don't start a war Dean," Donovan warned wondering if Butler was being a bit too enthusiastic.

"Yes sir. Just wanting to keep my options open if we run into trouble," Butler replied.

"And for you Mr. Donovan?" McInerney queried.

"A sidearm will suffice thanks. I am planning to keep a low profile until we find out what is going on."

Creighton turned to Butler and Owens. "You two will need to get moving if you are to get there and back today. It is quite a drive, and the road is not the best."

"Do you need directions?"

"The mine owner gave us a map," Owens said confirming the Americans could find their way.

Creighton shot a concerned glance at McInerney, "Two of our boys are overdue coming back from the mine. We are not expecting any trouble but keep an eye out for them."

"Yes sir," acknowledged Owens.

"McInerney will arrange trucks from the motor pool," Creighton said. "Bill, do you want someone to come with you to the port? It is safe enough, but you never know."

"I will be fine Peter, but thanks for the offer," Donovan replied.

"If there is nothing else, follow me gentlemen and we will get you kitted," McInerney said, directing the men towards the embassy's arsenal.

* * *

Donovan arrived at the port two hours later. The drive was along a dirt road following the mighty Congo.

The road was a popular spot for pop-up markets and Donovan took the time to pick up some local produce to snack on as well as souvenirs for his children. He resisted the temptation of buying them shrunken heads, opting instead for colourful straw dolls.

He parked in front of the port authority office and went in the main door where the port manager, Henri Goma, was doing paperwork.

"Can I help you?" Goma asked, surprised at having company that morning.

"Usually, our guests arrive from the ocean, not by road." He continued in his friendly manner.

"My name is Donovan. And you are?" The American replied politely.

"My name is Henri Goma. I am the port manager," Goma said introducing himself.

"My name is Bill Donovan, Mr. Goma. I am with the United States government. The Belgian Congo Mining Corporation has given its entire supply of uranium to my government. I am here to make sure we safely take possession and that it is loaded expeditiously."

"Do you have any identification Mr. Donovan?" Goma asked wanting to make sure he had his I's dotted and T's crossed, particularly given that Donovan was claiming to be a representative of the United States government. "We have loaded many shipments and have never had any issues. In fact, a shipment left port just the other day," he added trying to get across the message that the port of Matadi was a safe and secure location.

Donovan took the letter from Sangier out of his jacket pocket, as well as a letter of introduction from Secretary of State Cordell Hull. "Here you are Mr. Goma. This is a letter from the Belgian Congo Mining Corporation with shipping instructions in care of the United States government. Also, a letter of credentials from my government."

Goma read the letters and promptly gave them back to Donovan satisfied as to his bona fides.

Donovan continued, "I am sure your dock workers will do their best Mr. Goma. However, we are concerned about the safety of the cargo."

"Of course, Mr. Donovan," Goma replied, an expression of concern growing on his face.

"Our sources believe there may be interest from other parties, who shall we say, are not pleased that Mr. Sangier gave the ore to my government."

Goma asked, "Who exactly are you worried about Mr. Donovan? Piracy is part of life in Africa, but even the bravest pirates would be fools to pick a fight with the American government."

Not wanting to give too much away, Donovan changed subject. "Have there been any unusual visitors to the port Mr. Goma, or any ships arriving other than freighters that come through routinely?"

Thoughtfully, Goma replied, "Nothing out of the ordinary… but I did have a visit from a German consular official earlier in the week wanting information on ships transiting the port. He said he was acting on behalf of a German business that had its cargo stolen."

"What did you tell him?" Donovan asked with eyebrow raised.

"I gave him the list. I thought nothing of it," Goma said telling a white lie. He did not want to admit to the United States government that he had accepted a bribe for the information.

"Ok. What about ships transiting through the port, or scheduled into the port?" Donovan asked.

"Nothing out of the ordinary... except..."

"Yes Mr. Goma. Continue." Donovan said, noticing the pause.

"There is a freighter due into port in a couple of days. She is in transit to Cape Town but is having engine trouble. We had a message from her this morning."

"Where is she registered Mr. Goma and where is she coming from?" Donovan asked.

"She will present her papers when she arrives. Her name is the Hildebrand. She is out of Hamburg," Goma replied.

Having received the answer to the question he was seeking, Donovan was ready for a tour of the port. "Thank you, Mr. Goma. Can you show me where the uranium loads?"

"Of course, Mr. Donovan." They got into Donovan's truck and headed for the docks.

* * *

Owens and Butler were making good time on the way to the mine. Owens was driving while Butler navigated and road shotgun. They were about three hours into the drive, and it was midday. The sun was hot but there was a nice breeze generated by the speed of the topless Bedford. However, it was a humid day and there were lots of bugs hitting the windscreen in addition to the men.

Owens tried small talk to make the drive seem faster. "I hope I never get posted to this part of the world. It is a godforsaken place," he said swatting at mosquitos as they drove along the bumpy dirt road.

"Sure is," Butler agreed, but he was more focused on their safety. "There are a million places around here that we could get ambushed if someone wanted us out of the way."

Butler continually scanned the countryside for any sign of trouble.

"Or we could get trampled by a herd of elephants. Probably more likely," Owens said trying to lighten Butler's gung-ho demeanor.

Butler laughed. "Probably."

"How much further Dean?"

"Forty kilometres or so I think," he said looking at the map. "In about ten kilometres we are going to go over the train tracks then wind down to the river. After that it is straight ahead to the mine."

"We should check out the train tracks," Owens said thinking aloud. "If the Germans are going to hijack the shipment, taking the train would be a logical strategy."

"I agree," Butler said continuing to scan the landscape, "but let's get to the mine and ask the manager's opinion. We can check out the tracks on the way back."

* * *

The German spy and his two security guards were driving slowly along the train tracks looking for an ambush site. The jungle on either side of the tracks was as thick and unforgiving as it had been the day before when they did their initial reconnaissance.

Frustrated at the lack of opportunity provided by the dense jungle, Hofmayer moaned, "I doubt we are going to find a suitable site Meyer. The jungle is too thick, and we will not have time to jump onto the platform if the train is moving too fast."

"I agree Hofmayer," Meyer said, sharing the Abwehr agent's frustration at their slow progress along the vine covered railway tracks. "I think we should plan to either take the train closer to the port, or before it leaves the mine."

"Agreed." Hofmayer replied, thinking that the options the captain laid out made the most sense.

"Let's get onto the road and back to Leopoldville. We can check the tracks closer to the port tomorrow. If there is no viable location close to the port, then we will take the mine and wait for the train to come to us."

"Fischer, back to the road please," Meyer ordered. Needing no encouragement Fischer sped up to get to the next crossing.

* * *

Donovan completed his inspection of the port and was ready to drive back to Leopoldville. "Thanks for the tour, Mr. Goma. All looks good. Expect our ship in the next few days."

"Very good Mr. Donovan. If you need anything else, please call," Goma said wanting to be helpful to the United States.

"I will Mr. Goma," he said. "And you can call me at the Sabena Hotel in Leopoldville if you need to get hold of me." Donovan paused, then continued as an idea popped into his head. "You can do one thing for me."

"Anything for the United States government Mr. Donovan."

"When the German freighter arrives can you give her a birth on the opposite side of the port?" he asked. "I want to keep the Germans as far away as possible from the uranium."

"I will take care of it," Goma replied.

* * *

Back on the road to the mine Butler and Owens crossed the train tracks and followed the road as it merged with the river. They came across an overturned truck in the water. There were no signs of life.

"Pull over Nash. That truck looks British and has not been there very long."

Owens stopped their truck on the road next to the semi submerged vehicle. There were no weeds or other vegetation overgrowing the truck that would indicate it had been there for a long time. The truck also had no rust, so Butler concluded it had overturned recently.

They got out of their vehicle to inspect the wreck. Butler carried his shotgun out of caution.

"I think we have found out what happened to the missing soldiers," Owens said. "They must have been speeding and flipped the truck."

"Maybe, or they had some help," Butler suggested as he inspected the blown tires protruding from the undercarriage.

"Look at this Nash," Butler said pointing at one of the flat tires. "I do not see any rocks on the road that would lead to a blow-out like this. On top of that, what are the odds that both left-side tires would blow simultaneously?"

"Pretty slim I would have thought," Owens replied, agreeing with his military colleague's analysis.

Butler looked at the road to see if there was anything else that might have caused the accident, but it was flat and there was nothing lying nearby that could have damaged the tires. He could clearly see the tire tracks showing the truck had skidded off the road and into the river, flipping over as it lost control on the sloping riverbank.

Looking at the crocodiles and then the ground around the road, Owens said grimly, "I expect the crocodiles had a good dinner. There are no footprints near the truck. I think the poor bastards ended up in the river."

"This accident has murder written all over it," Butler added grimly. "We will radio the embassy when we get to the mine. It is not much further."

They got back into the truck and set off for the mine thinking to themselves that the opposition was likely to be close by, and in a murderous mood. Butler subconsciously pumped his shotgun, ensuring there was a slug in the firing chamber.

An hour later the men arrived at the mine. They stopped at the gate and were greeted by an armed guard.

"What is your business here gentlemen?" the guard asked not looking terribly interested in his duties.

"We are here to see the mine manager," Owens announced in an officious manner.

Nonchalantly the guard opened the gate. "Go straight ahead to the first building sirs. Mr. De Suter is in the office."

Owens and Butler drove through the gate and parked in front of the office. De Suter came out of his office having seen strangers at the gate. The mine did not receive many visitors, and this was the second day running.

"Can I help you?" he asked.

"Are you Mr. De Suter?" Owens asked, querying the middle-aged Belgian.

"I am. And you are?"

"Owens and Butler from the United States government. Mr. Sangier sends his regards," Owens replied.

Upon hearing Sangier's name De Suter smiled. He was visibly relieved, as he had not heard from his boss since the decision was made a few weeks prior to turn over the uranium resource to the Americans.

"So, he is safe?" De Suter asked.

"Yes, he and his family are on their way to the United States," Butler replied.

"He said to give you this," Butler continued, giving Sangier's letter to De Suter.

De Suter read the letter which satisfied him that the American's were who they claimed to be. "Please, come into the office. Can I offer you a refreshment?"

"A beer would go down well right now," Butler said feeling parched from the drive through the hot jungle. Owens nodded enthusiastically in agreement.

"With pleasure," De Suter replied.

The office was sparse but functional. It also had an air conditioner that was groaning in a losing effort to cool the room and a refrigerator containing cold beverages. In the Belgian Congo, these appliances were worth a gold bar each. "Please take a seat, gentlemen," De Suter said.

They sat down at the meeting table. On it was a map, sitting beneath a sheet of glass, displaying a geological survey of the mineral deposits in the region. De Suter served Owens and Butler a cold Belgian ale. "I am presuming you are here to make sure the uranium ships safely," he asked the men.

"That is correct," Owens replied, intently studying the map as it had much more detail than the version, he was given by Sangier. "A freighter is on its way and should be here in the next couple of days."

"Have you had any visitors Mr. De Suter, or seen anyone in the vicinity of the camp that looks out of place?" Butler asked.

"We don't get many visitors to the mine Mr. Butler," De Suter said. "As you can appreciate from your drive, visitors, other than the odd hunter or a local looking for a job, are a strange site as it is a long drive from Leopoldville."

De Suter added, "Yesterday, a couple of British soldiers were here asking the same questions and making sure our security was satisfactory. Why do you ask?"

"We think there are some German agents in country who will try to hijack the shipment," Owens replied seriously.

"I see. Edgar was worried about that, which is why he contacted the United States government. He hates the Nazis and was sure they would make a bomb if they got hold of the uranium," De Suter told the men. "He wants it as far away from Hitler as possible."

"What is so special about this mine?" Butler asked De Suter. "Our Canadian allies mine uranium. This is a long way to go given the available alternative."

De Suter replied, "Because the ore from this mine is almost pure Mr. Butler. It is also the 235 derivative which makes it very desirable to anyone generating nuclear power, and extremely dangerous for anyone making a bomb."

"You need less of this ore to make a bomb Mr. Butler," he continued. "Canadian uranium is around two percent pure while this vein is almost seventy five percent pure. When you do the maths, you can see why the ore from this mine is so desirable, particularly to a nasty group of thugs like the Nazis. You do not need much of it to inflict a lot of damage."

Owens nodded. "I see. Now I understand why our government wants it so badly."

"Maybe you should have studied geology Nash," Butler quipped.

"Why don't you stay the night gentlemen," De Suter said. "Driving back on that road is quite dangerous in darkness."

"To that point Mr. De Suter," Butler said. "We came across a truck, a few kilometres up the road, that had crashed into the river. It was overturned and there was no sign of life. It had not been there very long. We think the two British soldiers who were here yesterday, either had an accident or met with foul play. From what I can see it is probably the latter. Can you get a message to the British embassy letting them know?"

"I will take care of it," De Suter said looking concerned. "Let me get accommodation organized for you. We can talk more once you are settled in." He went outside and waved to a mine worker to come in.

"Jacob, can you please take these gentlemen to Mr. Sangier's quarters?" he instructed his employee.

"Yes sir. Please follow me gents."

"Let's have dinner at six. We can discuss the details of your plan then," De Suter said. "Edgar's quarters are air conditioned and have indoor plumbing, so you both should be comfortable."

Owens and Butler expressed their thanks for the hospitality and followed Jacob to their quarters.

CHAPTER SEVEN

CHANGE OF PLAN

Meyer, Fischer and Hofmayer drove back to Leopoldville without incident. The soldiers dropped the spy at his hotel. They had managed to miss the Americans, who had taken the main road along the river, while the Germans bumped along the train tracks.

"Pick me up in the morning at 8 a.m." Hofmayer ordered Meyer.

"I want to go to the port and then follow the railway back towards the mine. We need find a location to take the train that is closer to either Leopoldville or the port. If not, then we will simply take the mine," he continued, detailing his plan.

Meyer and Fischer confirmed they would return in the morning and then drove off.

Turning to the doorman, Hofmayer gave the middle aged uniformed black man, some money. "Arrange some feminine company for me this evening," Hofmayer said arrogantly and without discretion.

"Of course, Mr. Hofmayer. Was the last girl adequate?" the doorman asked looking stoically at the fat German.

"Yes, but she stayed too long," he replied, then gave the doorman some more money. "Tell her to bring a friend and make sure I am not disturbed."

"Certainly, sir," the doorman said dutifully, wondering to himself who was worse, the Germans or the Belgians.

Leaving the doorman to his duties, Hofmayer went to the reception desk to collect his key. He gave a disdainful look to a black man who was loitering near the hotel entrance.

"My key," Hofmayer said to the receptionist.

"Here you are sir," she said taking the key from its cubby hole. "Is there anything else you need?"

"Are there any messages?" Hofmayer asked. The receptionist pulled out a desk file that contained messages for guests.

"Yes, one sir," she said handing Hofmayer an envelope that had been left at the desk earlier that day. He took the message without opening it and went up the stairs to his room.

* * *

Donovan arrived in Leopoldville from Matadi later that afternoon. He went to the British embassy to dictate a report to go into the diplomatic pouch to the Foreign Office, and from there to the United States embassy in London and finally to Washington. The entire process would take at least a week, if not two, before President Roosevelt would read his report.

After that it was back to the hotel to shower, rest and change. As the sun set and the temperature cooled, he retired to the garden bar to enjoy a cold drink. A waiter came to his table carrying a telephone.

"Mr. Donovan sir? I have a telephone call for you. Reception will put it through." He left the phone on the table, and it rang straight away.

"Donovan speaking," he said answering the call.

"Mr. Donovan, this is Henri Goma."

"Yes Mr. Goma?"

"The ship from Hamburg is arriving tomorrow morning," Goma reported. "It is normal practice that I would board her, check her paperwork, and inspect for contraband, pests and such. Would you like to join me?"

"Very much so. I will be there at 8 a.m."

"I will meet you in my office," Goma replied. "In addition, the American freighter will be arriving late tomorrow or early the next day. She is making her way down the west coast. She radioed her position two hours ago."

"Very good. I will get word to the mine to begin preparing the shipment," he said thanking Goma for the news.

"I will see you in the morning Mr. Donovan."

* * *

Hofmayer was waiting for his feminine company to arrive when there was a knock on his door. The fat German promptly opened it expecting two local lovelies. Surprised, he was confronted by a tall, blond, white woman. Worse, he recognized her, and his carnal thoughts went promptly by the wayside.

"Fräulein Schuyler," Hofmayer said evenly trying to hide his surprise and irritation, greeting his attractive colleague from the Abwehr without enthusiasm. Together with his other faults, the German spy was also sexist, not believing women had a place in the spy business, or any other with the exception of the kitchen or laundry.

"What brings you to this part of the world?" He continued, now with an annoyed look on his face.

"May I come in?" Schuyler asked, amused at his discomfort. She thought her Abwehr colleague to be a buffoon, albeit a ruthless one, and wondered what on earth Canaris was thinking when he appointed Hofmayer to run the operation.

The big German stood aside and gestured for her to come into his room. "Of course. Please."

Schuyler entered the room and sat down. "You look surprised Hofmayer. Perhaps you were expecting someone else?" She said with the knowing smile of a spy who had done their due diligence before calling on a colleague.

She glanced at the unopened envelope on the desk where Hofmayer had discarded it. "If you had checked the message, you would have seen that I would be paying you a visit this evening," she said, teasing the fat German.

Recovering from his surprise, and ignoring her sarcasm, he retorted with his usual arrogance. "I was not expecting reinforcements fräulein Schuyler. I can assure you that all is under control."

"Perhaps, Hofmayer," Schuyler said in business-like fashion. "However, the Führer and Admiral Canaris are in no mood to tolerate a failure of this mission, so the admiral asked me to provide assistance."

"And what type of assistance does the admiral have in mind?" Hofmayer asked, irritated that his mission was in danger of being usurped, particularly by a woman.

Schuyler continued, "First, Hofmayer, there is the matter of the enemy agents."

"Enemy agents fräulein Schuyler?" he answered looking surprised. "We have not observed any enemy activity except for two nosy Brits, who we have taken care of."

"There are three American agents in or near Leopoldville," Schuyler reported. "They need to be eliminated. They arrived a few days ago and I expect they are at the mine. Tomorrow you will go to the mine and terminate them. Do I make myself clear?"

"Of course," he responded, regaining his enthusiasm with the order to assassinate enemies of the German state. "It will be my pleasure. I will leave first thing in the morning."

"If they do not arrive tomorrow, wait until they do." She continued firmly, wanting to make sure Hofmayer would not interfere with her part of the mission.

"Very well," Hofmayer replied, agreeing to his place in the mission. He thought to himself that when he took possession of the uranium, he would turn the tables on the upstart young woman and make her his subordinate. Two could play the politics game and whoever had control of the uranium would be king.

"The freighter Hildebrand arrives in the morning," she continued. "I will make sure she is not impeded loading the uranium."

Schuyler got up to leave. "Enjoy your evening Hofmayer," she said with a knowing look. "I will let myself out." She exited the room.

Hofmayer frowned and picked up the phone. "Put me through to the German embassy," he instructed the hotel operator.

The embassy receptionist answered. "Get Schmidt on the line," he said rudely.

Schmidt was working late and answered immediately. "Schmidt speaking."

"Schmidt, this is Hofmayer," he said getting straight to the point. "Have Meyer and Fischer pick me up in the morning at 6 a.m. We are going back to the mine. Tell them to bring provisions for three days."

"Yes, Herr Hofmayer. I will make sure they are there," he said. Hofmayer hung up the phone ignoring the usual pleasantries.

Five minutes later there was a knock at the door. The two attractive young black women had arrived. "Come in ladies," he said with a pleasing smile.

* * *

Owens, Butler and De Suter were discussing the details of shipping the uranium. The phone rang and it was Donovan on the other line. De Suter gave the phone to Owens.

"What's up Bill?" Owens asked Donovan.

"Our freighter will be in later tomorrow or early the next. Make sure the ore is loaded and ready Nash."

"Will do Bill," Owens replied. "We are staying the night at the mine and coming back first thing in the morning. Is there anything else?"

"Not for the moment," he said, deciding not to tell his men about the Hildebrand. "I will update you tomorrow."

Owens hung up the phone and returned to the discussion with the Belgian miner.

"When can you start loading the box cars Mr. De Suter?" Butler asked.

"Right away, assuming the freighter will be in port in the next few days," De Suter replied. "We have ample tonnage of ore ready."

"It will be. Bill just confirmed it will dock later tomorrow or early the next day," Owens said.

"Start getting the ore loaded," Butler instructed De Suter. "Also, let's get the train to the mine. I would rather have it here under armed guard."

"I will instruct the engineer to get the train ready, so you can bring it here at your convenience. It will take a couple of days to load the box cars," De Suter replied.

"How much ore is left to be extracted?" Owens asked.

"Many tons. The vein is still open Mr. Owens, and our geologists think it will extend at least two hundred metres yet," De Suter explained.

"Can you close the mine entrance?"

"How closed, Mr. Owens?"

"Enough so that the Germans or anyone else cannot access the vein," Owens stated.

"I will arrange to have the entrance sealed," De Suter replied, confirming his understanding that the Americans wanted the mine closed permanently. "I will take care of it once the train is loaded."

"Perfect," Owens said. "Hitler can choke on it."

Butler interjected. "Nash and I think the British soldiers were murdered by German agents. We also think they have been observing the camp's activities. Can you make sure you have enough security in place in case they try to hijack the train?"

"I will make the necessary arrangements," De Suter confirmed. He took a deep breath to relieve the tension he was suddenly feeling with the news that the German spies may have been responsible for killing the soldiers.

"Dean and I will accompany the train Mr. De Suter," Owens said. "But we need to get back to Leopoldville to arrange reinforcements. We will let you know when we are ready."

"Very well," De Suter said. Thinking about the possibility of German agents causing trouble, he added, "When you go back tomorrow, I suggest you drive along the train tracks for the first thirty or forty kilometres. Your truck is wider than the narrow rail gauge, so it should not be too bumpy. But anyone wanting to make trouble will do so along the river, as you found out earlier today. Once the road moves inland the jungle thins out and you will be much safer."

"Good idea," Butler agreed. "We will also be able to get a good look at the tracks and likely ambush sites."

"And avoid the fate of the British troopers," Owens said agreeing with his partner that the Germans were probably in the area and in a murderous mood.

"You crossed the tracks twice today," De Suter replied. "Get back onto the road at the second crossing."

"Good plan, although Dean is itching to use his new toys," Owens added on a lighter note, poking fun at his gun-toting partner.

"I expect I will get to soon enough," Butler replied seriously.

"Very good. I will leave you to your evening. Please join me in the morning for breakfast then you can get on your way," De Suter said bidding the men good night.

As the two Americans walked back to their quarters, Owens turned to his partner. "What do you think Dean?" he asked.

"I think it is time to hunt some Germans," Butler said with a determined look on his face. "If they were on the road today, they would have taken a shot at us. My guess is they have someone watching the camp and may be waiting for us tomorrow. Let's take our time getting back and see if we can surprise them."

"I won't be much help you know," Owens confessed, feeling useless, not knowing if he was capable of saving his own skin in a gun fight.

Butler smiled feeling sympathy for his friend and his upper-class upbringing, which did not prepare him for the life he was now living. "Just remember. Point the gun and spray the bullets. You are bound to get lucky." Yawning, he said, "Let's get a good night sleep and be up and out of here early." Butler pulled a coin out of his pocket. "I'll flip you for the bed."

* * *

Meyer and Fischer arrived at Hofmayer's hotel at sunrise the next morning and waited in the Kübelwagen for the Abwehr spy. The vehicle was again loaded with supplies for an extended stay in the jungle. A local, the same man that Hofmayer passed on his way into the hotel the previous evening, was standing on the sidewalk in front of the hotel keeping an eye on the entrance.

Hofmayer came out of the hotel promptly at 6 a.m. Thumping the hood of the vehicle with his fist, he said enthusiastically to the German soldiers, "Let's get going. We have spies to catch." The fat German's tryst the night before had left him in good spirits and ready for more action.

"Excellent," Meyer replied. "To the mine Fischer."

"Yes sir," Fischer replied and pulled the Kübelwagen onto the street. He put his foot on the gas peddle and they were soon speeding along the empty street in the direction of the main road south to the mine.

The black man watching the Germans walked into the hotel and went straight to the public phone booth. He called the British embassy and asked for Creighton.

Creighton was at work early as always. He put down his cup of tea and answered the phone. "Creighton speaking."

"It is Stephon, Mr. Creighton," the man said. "The German was picked up a moment ago by two men. They were dressed for hunting. They have weapons with them and a full load of supplies."

"Which direction did they go?" Creighton asked.

"South towards the main road out of Leopoldville, Mr. Creighton," Stephon replied.

"Thanks, old boy," he said then hung up the phone. He immediately called De Suter.

De Suter was in the office making a list of all that needed to be done to get the ore moving and the mine closed. "De Suter speaking."

"It is Creighton from the British embassy Mr. De Suter. We believe three German agents are on their way to the mine. They left their hotel in Leopoldville a few minutes ago and are heavily armed," Creighton warned the miner.

"Ok. I will let our American friends know," De Suter replied. He hung up the phone and immediately went to the mess to find Butler and Owens.

The Americans were having breakfast and De Suter joined them, pouring himself a cup of coffee. "Good morning, men. Creighton just called. He says we will be having company. Three German agents."

"When?" Butler asked with a deadly serious look.

"Creighton says they left the hotel in Leopoldville a few minutes ago. Five hours at a maximum," De Suter surmised after doing some mental arithmetic.

"Are they the same agents that killed the Brits?" Owen asked.

"Creighton didn't say, but we should assume so," De Suter said.

Butler thumped his fist on the table and turned to Owens. "Let's give them a taste of their own medicine Nash." Convinced the Germans were behind the killing of the two soldiers, Butler was determined to avenge the deaths of his military brothers.

Owens agreed but tried to caution his aggressive colleague. "Remember we are not at war Dean. We do not need a diplomatic incident with Hitler."

"That doesn't seem to stop the Nazis, Nash," Butler continued his early-morning rant. "They will murder whoever gets in their way to get what they want!"

There was an uncomfortable pause knowing the American's paths were about to cross with their adversaries and the rules of engagement were foggy at best. Taking a deep breath, Butler took a step back, knowing Owens was right. "Well, we can at least slow them down," he conceded. "It is a long walk back to Leopoldville. Lots of wild animals out there."

Butler looked at De Suter. "Do you have a hunting rifle with a scope?" he asked. "The Brits gave me an Enfield, but I could use a scope for the task at hand."

"Of course. You can borrow mine," De Suter offered.

"Where should we wait for our German friends?" Butler asked De Suter.

"I would find a spot near the second rail crossing," the Belgian replied without hesitation. "They will need to slow down to cross the tracks."

"We better get going Nash," Butler said to his reluctant comrade in arms. "It will take us a few hours to find an ambush site and get set up."

Butler turned to De Suter. "You better double the guard. Tell them to shoot first and ask questions later."

"I will see to it," he replied. "Good luck gentlemen and stay safe."

CHAPTER EIGHT

LET THE GAMES BEGIN

E arly that same morning, Donovan arrived at the port to inspect the German freighter. Standing outside the office, Goma greeted Donovan. "Good morning Mr. Donovan. The Hildebrand has arrived. She came in a few hours ago." He gave Donovan a hat, badge, and clipboard. "Officially you are with Belgian customs."

"I will do my best to look officious," Donovan said dryly, putting on the hat and pinning the badge to his shirt, continuing to be impressed with Goma's hutzpah.

"I'll follow your lead," the American confirmed with a more serious note in his voice.

Donovan followed Goma along the dock in the direction of the Hildebrand. Arriving at the freighter's birth Goma called to a sailor who was on watch on the main deck.

"Ahoy. I am the port manager," Goma called out. "We are here to inspect your ship and cargo. Permission to come aboard."

"One moment. I will get the captain," the sailor replied and disappeared to collect the captain. A minute or so later the captain appeared on deck.

"I am Captain Heitz. What is your business here?" the ship's senior officer called down to Goma.

"Just routine captain," Goma replied. "We inspect all ships entering the port."

"Come aboard," he waved to the men to board the ship. Donovan and Goma went up the gang plank where the captain was waiting for them.

"What is the purpose of docking at Matadi?" Goma asked the captain.

"We are on our way to Cape Town and have engine troubles. We are in for repairs," Heitz replied, sticking to the story he was given by the Abwehr.

Goma nodded feigning disinterest. "Your manifest please, captain."

"It is on the bridge. However, we are running empty. We are on our way to pick up cargo in South Africa. This way gentlemen," the captain said. Donovan and Goma followed Heitz to the bridge.

"I will inspect the cargo hold Mr. Goma. I can find my way," Donovan said as he left the group and walked towards the staircase leading to the hold.

Heitz motioned to a sailor. "Please accompany the customs inspector Kornheizer." The young sailor followed Donovan to the hold. He was armed with a rifle and side arm which Donovan thought a bit odd, as there was no reason for the merchant ship's sailors to fear for their safety. And given the hold was empty, there was nothing to steal.

Donovan was counting the crew and trying to assess their capabilities to defend the ship as he made his way out of the staircase and along the corridor to the cargo bay. He was also trying to figure out the best way to disable the large vessel. He quickly concluded that the Hildebrand had too many sailors on board, many who were armed, to be able to take, or damage the ship without a lot of blood being shed.

As he arrived at the hold, a tall, attractive blond woman approached Donovan. "May I be of assistance?" she asked him suspiciously. She spoke with a heavy German accent.

Donovan looked up at the blond, guessing from the description Owens and Butler had provided, that she was the German spy they had run across in Lisbon. "Just a routine inspection madam. And you are?" he asked blandly, being careful not to give the impression that he knew, or cared, who she was.

"I am with the German embassy," she announced curtly.

Donovan replied officiously, "I am with Belgian customs. We inspect all ships entering port."

Convinced she was being conned, Schuyler observed suspiciously, "You don't sound Flemish, mister...?"

Donovan ignored her observation. "And you do not look like a sailor, miss...? Now mind your business and let me finish my inspection."

He walked away from her and opened one of the cargo bay doors to confirm it was empty.

"Schuyler," she called after him. "Our Führer will not appreciate colonial interference with the Fatherland's business," she threatened, glaring at Donovan.

Now annoyed, Donovan decided to pick an argument with the spy.

"You are a long way from Germany Miss Schuyler," Donovan said issuing a vailed threat of his own.

"And unless you want this ship quarantined you will get out of my way," he followed with a direct threat.

Schuyler scowled, backing off. "I hope we will meet again, Herr customs inspector or whoever you really are. Perhaps the circumstances will be different." She turned around and exited the hold, leaving Donovan to complete his inspection.

Donovan turned to the sailor. "Kornheizer is it? I have seen enough. Take me to the bridge."

They walked back to the main deck and ran into Goma, the captain, and the Abwehr agent.

"Was the inspection satisfactory?" Goma asked, communicating an air of authority. "Here is the manifest," he said handing the document to Donovan.

"All is in order Mr. Goma. The ship is empty as the captain stated," Donovan reported, while glancing at the manifest to again give the impression that the business of the day was official. Turning to the Germans, Goma instructed, "As you are an unscheduled guest, and I have other shipping to accommodate, you have seventy-two hours to complete your repairs and be on your way. For your own safety, no one is to leave the ship."

Heitz protested the order. "We need parts to repair the engine and purchase provisions for the rest of the voyage."

"Make a list of everything you need, and I will see to it," Goma said officiously. "However, you must follow my instructions, or I will have the local police enforce my order."

"I will take care of it," the captain conceded, clearly unhappy about being restricted to the ship but thinking better of having the colonial Belgian police barricade the freighter.

Goma smiled. "Very good."

The captain then pointed at the blond woman. "Fräulein Schuyler is our country's diplomatic representative. I take it she can leave the ship?"

"Of course," Goma said dismissing any notion of respect for her diplomatic status. "Good day."

Donovan and Goma walked down the gang plank leaving the captain and the Nazi spy to consider their next steps.

The men walked back towards the port office. "Anything interesting Mr. Donovan?" Goma asked.

"Just an empty hold…" he said not wanting to raise his concerns to Goma about fräulein Schuyler. "And every sailor I passed was carrying a weapon. That is quite a lot of fire power for a merchant ship. Is that normal for ships arriving here?"

"Not at all Mr. Donovan. Most ships have lookouts, but the area is quite safe, and we have our own security at the port," he said, then added, "The Belgian government also polices Matadi with an iron fist."

Goma raised an eyebrow. "And the woman? I doubt she is who she said she was."

"Yes, I expect you are right," Donovan said vaguely, again being impressed with Goma's judgement.

The men arrived back at the office and Donovan climbed into his truck. He had seen enough and wanted to get back to the British embassy so he could prepare another progress report for Knox.

"Be careful Mr. Goma. She looks dangerous," Donovan warned the port manager, circling back to the subject of the spy.

"Yes Mr. Donovan. I will post an armed guard at the gate and ensure the police stop by regularly," Goma said agreeing with Donovan's assessment then adding, "I think I will also wear a side arm while that ship remains in port."

"Very prudent, Mr. Goma," thinking out loud, Donovan asked, "Can you arrange a power outage at the port, Mr. Goma?"

"Just let me know when Mr. Donovan." Goma confirmed, assuming that the Americans were planning to make the Germans' lives a misery.

"I will call you when my colleagues return," Donovan said now deep in thought. He bid Goma farewell, fired up the truck and drove off.

* * *

Butler and Owens left the mine immediately after breakfast and drove up the train tracks until they reached the second rail crossing on the Shinkolobwe road. They found a vantage point providing good visibility of the crossing as well as cover from their presumed German adversaries. Owens parked the truck underneath the jungle canopy and out of sight from the road. He pointed the vehicle in the direction of the rail crossing so they could retreat at speed if the battle went against them.

To make doubly sure that the Germans would slow down at the crossing, the Americans hacked down a large fern and put it across the road just past the tracks. They were ready and waiting for the Abwehr agents.

While the genesis of their mission was Butler's anger at the thought of the Nazis murdering the British soldiers and his desire to dish out some jungle justice, he had climbed down from his moral high ground and had convinced himself that the goal was to use force to dissuade the Germans from attempting to steal the uranium. He reasoned that some well placed bullets would knock the enthusiasm out of the German spies. Essentially, he and Owens would be standing up to the playground bully.

Butler had De Suter's hunting rifle at the ready and the scope calibrated on a tree near the point where they expected the Germans to slow down. The bolt action rifle was loaded with 30.06 cartridges which were powerful enough to bring down an elephant. Butler had more than enough fire power to plunder the Germans' vehicle. He also had a box of grenades courtesy of the British embassy's ammunition store, and his trusty shotgun just in case.

With a bit of effort—and trial and error—Owens managed to get the Bren set up on its tripod. Butler gave him another lesson on using the weapon, and Owens fired practice rounds into the river. The Harvard graduate, and State Department desk officer, was as ready for combat as he could be at short notice.

Lying in the jungle Owens was studying the ambush site through high-powered binoculars. He was happy with the set up. "That tree should slow them down a bit," he said optimistically to Butler.

"I expect so," Butler agreed. "They will have to slow down for the crossing and then again to get past the tree."

"And if they don't?" Owens asked, always the worry wart.

"You better hope that I am a good shot because we will have no chance to catch them if they get past us," Butler replied.

"When do you think they will be here?" Owens asked.

"Not too long I expect," Butler said looking at his watch. "As soon as I shoot out the tires, you open fire. Aim above their heads."

He couldn't resist teasing Owens. "Keep your head down in case they shoot back."

A look of shock crept across the young diplomat's face. Owens truthfully had not thought about the prospect that the Germans would return fire.

The jungle was filled with strange sounds which were unnerving for the two men. Butler, the professional soldier, tried to soothe his partner's nerves as Owens, now paranoid, was continually looking around, convinced that a wild animal would attack at any moment. "Easy Nash," Butler said. "We will be out of here soon enough. Besides, most animals are active at night and spend their days sleeping."

"Are you sure about that Dean?" Owens replied nervously, not convinced by Butler's theory.

"Absolutely," he replied, lying to his jumpy colleague in hopes of keeping him calm. "But you need to focus on what is in front of us. The Germans are a greater and more tangible threat than your run-of-the-mill lion or tiger."

Butler also wanted to make sure his partner was only thinking about the Nazi spies.

"I am not so sure," Owens replied failing to be convinced.

* * *

It was almost midday, and the Germans were well on the road to their camp. Hofmayer was sitting in the back of seat of the Volkswagen and starting to fidget. It was a long drive to the mine, and he was not a patient man. His large body also meant he was squeezed uncomfortably into the back seat of the Kübelwagen.

"Let's go to the same observation point as last time," Hofmayer ordered the soldiers.

"Yes sir," Fischer acknowledged.

Meyer, thinking aloud, said, "Once we see where the Americans are we will work out how to eliminate them. It will not be difficult. There is virtually no security at the mine to reinforce them."

Ignoring Meyer's attempt at small talk, Hofmayer asked impatiently, "how much further Fischer?"

"About forty kilometres, an hour or so," Fischer replied as he kept the Kübelwagen bouncing along the dirt track.

"I want to get this done today." Hofmayer said to the soldiers. He again shifted uncomfortably in the back seat and subconsciously tapped his fingers on the side of the topless Volkswagen, now even more anxious to get to their destination and take care of the Americans.

"The miners will be loading the uranium any day now, if they haven't already started, and the Americans are a complication we don't need," he continued, now acknowledging Meyer's earlier comment that eliminating the Americans would be their first priority.

"How do you know there are three of them Hofmayer?" Meyer asked, wondering where the intelligence originated from and if it was accurate.

"Abwehr has been monitoring their movement, captain. One of our agents spotted them in Lisbon before they boarded a plane to the Congo. I assure you the information is correct," he said, in his standard arrogant manner, not particularly caring what his underlings thought.

"What about the Brits?" Meyer asked. "They are obviously in on the mission."

"They pose no threat Meyer," Hofmayer replied with his usual overconfidence. "We dealt with them the other day and we will do so again if they get in our way."

Still fidgeting, and as if to reinforce his point, Hofmayer picked up his rifle, took aim, and blasted a hole in a large tree fifty metres in front of them.

* * *

Several minutes later, Owens was watching the road through his binoculars. He had taken on observer duties, in return for Butler agreeing to watch their sixes for wild animals. He saw a vehicle approaching north of the train tracks.

"Vehicle approaching Dean," Owens announced with nervous excitement.

Butler turned and looked up the dirt road at the approaching vehicle. "Ok. It must be them. I see three white men in a funny-looking truck. As soon as they slow down, I will shoot out their tires. Open-up with the Bren to keep their heads down," Butler said, reminding Owens of the plan of attack.

"Make sure you shoot over their heads, Nash." Butler again nagged his nervous partner. He wanted to be doubly sure that the objective was to leave the Germans alive, but worse for wear. As a military man Butler knew from experience that once the shooting started, the rules were quickly forgotten, or thrown out entirely.

The Germans' Kübelwagen, the funny-looking truck, approached the tracks and slowed down. Butler took aim with De Suter's hunting rifle. The vehicle crossed the tracks and slowed as Fischer spied the large fern blocking part of the road.

"Go around it, sergeant. You have room," Hofmayer ordered Fischer.

"Yes sir." Turning slowly, Fischer maneuvered the Kübelwagen to miss the fallen tree.

The vehicle was now almost stationery, so Butler adjusted his aim and shot the rear tire which exploded from the force of the massive bullet. "Now!" he yelled, commanding Owens to open fire.

Butler took aim and shot out the front tire forcing Fischer to hit the brakes. The Kübelwagen had come to a complete halt.

Owens pulled the trigger on the Bren. Nothing happened. "What the...?" Owens said to no one in particular, while frantically trying to get the gun to do its job.

"Take the safety off!" Butler yelled at Owens, who, in the excitement of the shooting, had forgotten the earlier instructions he had been given.

Owens flipped the safety and opened fire on the truck, shooting barely over the heads of the Nazi occupants. He adjusted his fire and put a second burst well over their heads.

"Out of the truck! Take cover and return fire!" Meyer yelled to his colleagues as he recovered his composure from the surprise attack. He ducked and rolled out the door placing the Kübelwagen between himself and their adversaries.

"Where are they?" Hofmayer yelled as he jumped out of the back seat and rolled away from the gunfire, landing next to Meyer.

"In the jungle across the road. Shoot there!" Meyer commanded, pointing roughly in the direction he believed the Americans were hiding. All three returned fire wildly.

The Americans continued to press their advantage as Owens kept the Germans' heads down with the machine gun. Butler reached into his bag for a grenade. Bullets were hitting around and above him but not close enough to do any damage.

"Keep your head down and run as soon as I hit them with the grenades. Fire up the truck and wait for me," Butler ordered Owens.

"Right!" Owens yelled excitedly. He kept his head down to duck the German bullets that were now targeting him. Getting ready to run for it, Owens took the Bren off its tripod, raised it above his head and fired wildly at the Kübelwagen.

Butler pulled the safety pin from a grenade and threw it towards the Germans. The grenade hit the road short of the Kübelwagen, then rolled underneath the disabled vehicle.

"Now!" he yelled at Owens. Owens got up and ran in a crouched position, crashing wildly through the jungle towards the train tracks where the truck was hidden. He tripped on an exposed tree root and fell head-first into the thick undergrowth. A bullet ripped through his shirt sleeve as he fell.

"Fuck," he cursed as he pulled himself off the jungle floor and stumbled over the train tracks, making it to the truck. He took off the tree branches serving as camouflage and started the engine.

Hofmayer looked up to see the grenade rolling under the Kübelwagen, and dove into the ditch on the opposite side of the road, just barely getting out of the way. "Grenade!" he yelled to his comrades as he rolled. Ironically, he ended up lying uncomfortably next to the bank of the crocodile-infested Congo river.

The grenade exploded under the chassis of the vehicle, lifting the Kübelwagen off the ground and igniting the gas tank. It was destroyed and burning out of control. Most of the provisions they had brought with them were also engulfed in flames. The two German soldiers rolled clear of the explosion but were hit by debris.

A crocodile hoping to feast on the fat German slithered into the river and swam menacingly close to Hofmayer's position. The Nazi spy, seeing the massive beast coming his way, moved surprisingly quickly for a big man. He scampered up the riverbank and crawled back onto the road, taking up position with his battered and bruised colleagues behind the smoldering vehicle. Meyer and Fischer continued to counterattack the Americans, firing into the jungle close to Butler's position.

Butler stayed on the attack. He threw another grenade then retreated to the truck. The grenade exploded near the wrecked Kübelwagen, forcing the Germans to keep their heads down.

Butler wasted no time getting into the truck. "Get us out of here Nash!"

Owens gunned the engine and drove off, bouncing the poor truck along the train tracks. They hit the crossing at speed and veered north on the road back to Leopoldville.

"Good work buddy!" cried an adrenalin-pumped Butler, slapping Owens on the back.

Seeing the truck accelerate onto the main road, Hofmayer took aim and shot at it, shattering the windscreen. "I will see you again American bastards!" he shouted angrily at his retreating foes.

Owens was surprised by the bullet shattering the windscreen and briefly lost control of the steering wheel. "Shit!" he yelled as the truck swerved, then got back online as he regained control.

"Steady, we will be out of range in a tick," Butler said encouraging Owens not to panic now the battle had been won. He turned around and returned fire at the Germans, shooting wildly from the rapidly moving vehicle.

"If the Germans didn't know they had competition, they do now," Butler laughed as the two were now well clear of the ambush site and out of harm's way.

* * *

The return journey was without event, and Owens and Butler arrived at the hotel a few hours later. Donovan was sitting outside enjoying the tropical evening with a cold beverage, watching a large snake several metres away gorge itself on an unsuspecting rat. Such was life at one of the finest hotels in the Congo in August 1939. Butler and Owens, looking worse for wear from their adventure earlier in the day, also turned up in search of a cold drink.

Donovan asked dryly, "You two have a busy few days?"

"We ran into our German friends Bill. They have a long walk home," Butler replied, understating the damage inflicted on the Germans.

"Good. I take it they are still alive?" He asked.

"I think so. They were still shooting at us as we retreated," Owens said, still looking out of sorts from his first military action.

Donovan nodded. "You better ring De Suter. Give him an update and get his men to keep an eye out for the Germans. Hopefully, they will give up, but some how I doubt it."

"I will do. Any news Bill?" Owens asked.

"Quite a bit. The German freighter arrived early this morning and another Nazi has joined the club," Donovan reported. "Tall blond woman. I expect the same one you met in Lisbon."

Butler nodded. "There cannot be more than one of her. What is she doing here?"

"She claims to a diplomat. She was on the German freighter while Goma and I were inspecting her this morning. Our freighter will be in tomorrow or early the next day," he said continuing the update. "Let's get the uranium loaded. I want you two to guard the train."

"What do you want to do about the German freighter?" Butler asked Donovan.

"I think we need to slow her down," Donovan said. He had spent most of his day, without success, thinking what his team could do to achieve that goal. "I want to make sure if we don't get the uranium, the Germans are in no position to get it out of the country, and that freighter is their only hope," Donovan reasoned. "If this mission ends in a draw, it will not be the worse news for our side. We will be able to get more resources down here to have another crack at it. Roosevelt is all in on this and has no intention of finishing second to the nutty Kraut."

With enthusiasm Butler chimed in. "Can we sink her sir?"

"Let me think about that," Donovan replied. "Why don't you two get cleaned up and we can continue the discussion over dinner."

Owens and Butler got up and went back to their rooms for a well-deserved shower and change of clothes.

An hour later and having recovered from their adventure earlier in the day the men were discussing their plan to get the uranium out.

"Goma called a half hour ago," Donovan said with a further update. "Our freighter will be in port tomorrow, so I want to get the uranium moving from the mine tomorrow as well. If we can do that, we will be able to get the freighter loaded and out of here within twenty-four hours or forty-eight max."

"I will let De Suter know after dinner. They started loading yesterday so it should be ready tomorrow, or the next day at the latest," Owens replied.

"Good. But tell him I want it loaded tomorrow, even if they must work all night," Donovan said firmly. "Let's focus on getting the ore to the port and after that we can figure out what we do about the German freighter. I want you two to escort the train to the mine first thing in the morning," Donovan said, continuing to issue orders. "I will get the Brits to send some troops to babysit our ship and make sure the Germans don't try and sabotage her."

"Do you think the Nazis will try anything Bill?" Butler asked Donovan.

"I expect so," he said instinctively. "An empty German freighter in port is no coincidence and this place is slack on security. It would only take a handful of men to take the port. The Hildebrand alone has more than enough men and weapons to do so."

The timetable that was unfolding forced Donovan to make up his mind. "Let's hit the Hildebrand once you two are back from the mine, and before our freighter finishes loading." He then cautioned his gung-ho underlings, "but just enough damage to keep her in port."

"Blowing a hole in her side will be difficult if not impossible," Butler said thinking through the practicalities of attacking the large ship.

"And boarding her to damage the engines will also be next to impossible given just about every sailor on board is carrying a weapon. They are expecting trouble and are prepared for it," Donovan said, ruling out that course of action.

"What about her propellers?" Owens asked trying to keep up with the two military types.

"We call them screws Nash. What do you have in mind?" Butler asked.

Owens continued, "If we damage them, they won't be able to get very far."

"Nowhere at all," Butler said, acknowledging Owens' good idea. "They will need to repair them before they can get off the dock. What do you think Bill? I can dive, I just need equipment and explosives."

Donovan agreed. "I will get what you need from the Brits. A small block of explosives with magnesium fuses should work. I will get Goma to cut the power at twenty-two hundred and turn on the emergency siren," he continued, explaining the plan that was developing. "You two can cut through the fence opposite the Hildebrand and Dean can get into the water near her stern. The noise from the siren should muffle the explosion." Donovan got the waiter's attention so he could sign for the meal. "We have work to do gentlemen," Donovan concluded. "Dean, get the truck and let's visit Creighton. Nash, call the mine and make sure the train will be ready to go first thing in the morning."

CHAPTER NINE

THE BATTLE OF SHINKOLOBWE

Hofmayer, Meyer and Fischer had survived the attack and spent an uncomfortable afternoon walking towards the mine. No traffic had driven by to help so the men camped in the jungle a few kilometres from the mine.

Early the next morning, they resumed their trek along the main road. Hofmayer was limping noticeably, his left ankle sprained, while the other two men were bandaged from various superficial wounds.

"How far captain?" Hofmayer asked grumpily.

"About five kilometres," Meyer replied.

"They will all suffer," Hofmayer scowled. "I can promise you there will be no witnesses when I am done. We will take the mine and wait for the Americans to come to us. Then I will have my revenge," he hissed with venom in his voice.

* * *

Owens and Butler were dropped off at the train by Donovan at 6 a.m. Both men were showing signs of wear from their encounter with the Germans the day before. Thankfully, the hotel had provided them with a thermos of coffee and a box of sandwiches to keep them going.

The train was pulled by an old steam engine dating to the turn of the century, but it was well maintained by the mining company and the engineer had made the run many times. The only appendage to the engine was a coal car. The box cars were at the mine being loaded with ore.

"Get it back safely gentleman," Donovan said to Butler and Owens, shaking their hands as they climbed onto the engine.

"Ready sirs?" the engineer asked. He was a fifty-something black man with leathered skin. His stoker was shovelling coal into the furnace to give the engine maximum power for the journey.

"Let's get going," Owens replied, all business.

The engineer pulled the steam whistle and put the train in gear.

"How long is the ride?" Owens asked the engineer.

"All going well, about five hours," he replied. "If the load is ready, we will hook up and come straight back. It will be much slower coming back as we will be carrying several tons of ore."

Butler took the opportunity to get some kip. "Keep an eye on things Nash. I am going to take a nap."

"What? No rock, paper, scissors?" Owens protested with good humour, but it was too late. Butler was snoring fitfully, stretched out on the floor at the rear of the engine. Owens poured himself a cup of coffee, picked up Butler's shotgun and took first watch.

* * *

At the mine, De Suter was supervising as his crew loaded the uranium into box cars. The men had worked all night at Donovan's request and the job was almost finished. An old steam shovel with a large scoop was dumping the ore into box cars. The ore was transported from the mine to the loading area in carts pulled by an old tractor and dumped next to the steam shovel. Despite being a valuable resource the process of extracting and getting the uranium to port was far from modern age.

A mine worker approached De Suter. "A message from the British embassy sir. The train is on its way and misters Owens and Butler are on it."

"Very good. We have about five hours so we should be ready. Have the explosives been set?" De Suter asked.

"Not yet Mr. De Suter," the miner replied.

"Send a team to the mine and get them planted. Evacuate the mine. There will be no more work to do once the train leaves," De Suter said issuing instructions to close the mine permanently.

Satisfied that his workers were doing their best to carry out his instructions, De Suter walked back to his office to begin packing.

* * *

Later that morning Hofmayer, Meyer and Fischer approached the front gate at the mine. They were carrying hunting rifles and a lone duffle bag, containing what was left of the supplies that had not been destroyed by the Americans. They were met by an armed guard. The gate was locked, and the guard was inside the fence. The second guard De Suter had posted was taking a break when the Germans arrived.

"Can I help you? Are you lost?" The guard asked, looking at the disheveled men in front of him.

"We were hunting, and our truck overturned five kilometres back," Hofmayer lied. "We need to call our hotel to get someone to pick us up."

"Wait here," the guard, a young black man, said cautiously, having been told by De Suter there could be German agents nearby. "I will get someone to call for you. What is the name of the hotel?"

Pointing his gun at the young guard, Hofmayer took charge. "Put your gun down and open the gate." The guard did as he was told, fear gripping his face as he fumbled with the padlock to open the gate.

"Fischer. Disarm our friend," Hofmayer commanded. "Meyer. You and Fischer assume guard duty. No one in or out."

Fischer frisked the guard, picked up his rifle, gagged and tied him up using the man's bootlaces, and moved him into the bush out of sight of anyone inside De Suter's office.

"What is your plan Hofmayer?" Meyer asked not knowing what was going through the spy's murderous mind.

"When the train arrives, I expect the Americans to be on it. Let them come into the mine office. I will take it from there. Just make sure there are no interruptions," he said to his subordinates.

Hofmayer entered the camp and walked the short distance to the mine office. He barged through the door, gun first, where De Suter was conferring with one of his staff.

Surprised at the intrusion, De Suter confronted Hofmayer. "Who are you and what do you want?"

Hofmayer pointed his gun and shot the staff member in the head, gruesomely making his point to De Suter that he would do as the German commanded if he valued his life. The staff member collapsed, falling into a heap in front of De Suter's desk. He was dead before he hit the ground.

"I am here for the uranium of course," Hofmayer said calmly. "Now put your hands on the desk and no sudden moves or you will meet the same fate as your colleague."

De Suter tried to regain his composure, looking at Hofmayer with disgust. "You won't get away with this whoever you are."

Hofmayer laughed at De Suter. "I am the one with the gun, Herr Miner."

With his gun pointed at De Suter, Hofmayer pulled out a rope and gag from his duffle bag and tied the manager to a chair. He dragged De Suter into the corner of the office, gagged him, and then sat down at his desk to wait for his next victim.

"Let's be comfortable, shall we?" he said smugly to De Suter. "I am sure your American friends will be along soon. My complements on having the ore ready for me."

He smiled arrogantly, knowing he was in command of the situation. De Suter grunted in annoyance at being bested by the Nazi.

* * *

Owens and Butler were standing watch on the train as it made its way to the end of the first leg of its journey. Both had benefited from a couple of hours of sleep on the way.

"How much longer?" Butler asked the engineer.

"We should be at the mine in a half hour," the engineer replied.

"Slow down before we get there. I am going to get off and have a look around," Butler ordered.

"Good idea Dean," Owens said to Butler. "The Germans won't be far away I expect."

"I agree…" Butler said feeling nervous about the uncertainty of the situation. He knew the Nazis would be in a foul mood if they were anywhere near the camp, given the treatment they had received the day before. While he hoped their ambush might have discouraged the spies from trying to take the uranium, he doubted they would give up easily. But where would they strike?

* * *

With the office under control, Hofmayer went outside and signaled Meyer to come into the camp. Meyer walked up to the office where Hofmayer was waiting on the front porch.

"Any issues?" Meyer asked.

"None for the moment Meyer," he replied. He pointed at the loading area a hundred or so metres away, where the ore was being shovelled into the box cars. Men were milling about unaware that the Germans had taken control of the camp. The loading area was surrounded by dense jungle effectively screening the view from the rail spur to the entrance of the camp. "I expect the train will be here momentarily given the box cars are just about full," Hofmayer observed.

Mayer agreed. "What are your orders?"

"If the Americans turn up at the gate, let them in," Hofmayer commanded. "Act is if you are security for the mine. They will come into the office, and I will be waiting. If, on the other hand, the Americans are on the train they will come to the office to see the manager. Either way I am ready."

"What if they recognize us from our encounter yesterday? Meyer asked.

"Then kill them." Hofmayer ordered.

"Ok," Meyer said finding no fault with Hofmayer's assumptions.

"And Meyer?"

"Yes Herr Hofmayer?"

"Kill anyone else approaching the gate," Hofmayer said with a dark look.

"Of course," Meyer replied nonplussed at the shoot first order. Turning around he walked back to the gate wondering if things would go as smoothly as Hofmayer anticipated.

* * *

The train approached the mine and slowed down to let Butler off. "Go to the office when we get there Nash. Let De Suter know we will take the ore that is ready now. I do not want to wait around and give the Germans an opportunity to hijack the train." Butler climbed onto the stair of the engine. "I am getting off here." De Suter's hunting rifle was strapped to his back, and he had a half-dozen grenades in a pouch at his side. He was wearing a sidearm, he had a hunting knife tucked into his boot and his trusty shotgun was hidden on the train just in case. Butler was ready for anything the Germans could throw at him. Or so he thought.

"Looks like the ore is loaded and ready to go," Owens observed looking through his binoculars at the mostly full box cars.

"Good. See you shortly buddy," Butler said as he jumped off the engine and bounded into the jungle.

The engine approached the rail spur a few minutes later. "Get the box cars hooked up and wait for us," Owens ordered the engineer. "Don't leave until Butler and I are aboard."

"Yes Mr. Owens. I need to fill the engine with water so we will be a little while," the engineer replied, going about his business.

The train pulled up to the loading point and Owens jumped off. The engineer parked on a turntable and was rotated by a mechanical gear shift that pointed it back towards Leopoldville. The engineer reversed the engine, backing it up until the mine workers waved at him to halt as the coal car coupled to the lead box car.

Owens walked to the office. Hofmayer was sitting behind the desk with gun pointed as he came through the door.

Owens' face dropped as he recognized, too late, that he had walked straight into a trap. De Suter was tied up in the corner of the office and a dead man was lying on the floor in front of the desk. Bile welled up in the young diplomat's mouth from the sight of death and he had to resist vomiting.

"Who are you?" Owens asked Hofmayer nervously.

"The competition, Herr…?" Hofmayer said with a look of satisfaction on his face as he completed the formalities.

"Owens," was the scratchy reply from the diplomat who was quickly running out of bravado. "And you won't get away with whatever you are planning, whoever you are." Fear was rushing up his spine, knowing he was helpless and out of his depth to deal with the situation.

"Put your hands on your head," Hofmayer commanded as he got up from the desk. Owens did as he was told, and the German frisked the diplomat pulling out a handgun he had tucked into his belt.

"Sit down," Hofmayer ordered, aggressively pushing Owens into the chair and tying him up. "If you move, I will shoot both you and the miner. If you cooperate you might live," he said with a sadistic smile. "Now tell me where your American friends are?"

"Fuck off you Nazi piece of shit," Owens retorted, surprising himself with his guttural response. Hofmayer retaliated, hitting Owens viciously across the jaw with the butt of his gun. Owens lost consciousness and slumped into the chair.

Pleased the situation was well under control, Hofmayer ripped the telephone off the wall, cutting off the mine's link to the outside world.

The German went outside and waved at Meyer to come into the mining office. "You and Fischer go to the train. We will be leaving shortly. Kill anyone that gets in your way, except the engineer, unless you know how to drive a steam engine."

"Yes Hofmayer," Meyer said, then saw Fischer waving at him in the distance. "Hold on. There is something going on at the gate."

Looking back at the gate, they could see a truck approaching with four men in it, three of whom were soldiers. "First things first Meyer. Get rid of that truck," Hofmayer barked. Meyer ran back to the gate to help Fischer, while Hofmayer retreated into the office to guard his insurance policies.

Donovan, McInerney and two soldiers were on their way to reinforce the mission. Donovan's sixth sense told him that trouble was brewing, and with the American freighter not yet in port, he decided to drive to the mine and lend a hand.

"Pull up at the gate, driver," Donovan ordered, spying what he thought was a guard manning the entrance. To his right he could see steam billowing above the trees but not the engine itself, as the train was hidden behind the thick jungle. "Looks like the train has arrived. No sign of Butler or Owens though," he said to the group.

"Your boys will be here somewhere," McInerney replied confidently.

Suddenly the guard opened fire on the truck. The driver swerved and hit the brakes, bringing the truck to a screaming halt. The trooper in the front passenger seat was hit in the shoulder and slumped over in pain.

"Everyone out!" McInerney said taking charge. The men rolled out of the truck and took cover behind the vehicle. McInerney dragged the wounded soldier out of the truck and into cover with the others.

"Looks like we have company Lt. Colonel," Donovan said, his voice hitting a higher pitch out of both fear and excitement.

Needing no encouragement, McInerney asked, "Permission to return fire Mr. Donovan," respecting the chain of command on the mission.

"Give them hell McInerney!" Donovan commanded as he drew his handgun and returned fire. McInerney and the driver opened-up with their weapons but the men were pinned down by the well-armed Germans. Meyer had joined the fight and taken up position on the opposite flank, between the train and the soldiers, keeping Donovan's team pinned behind the truck. The Germans had Donovan and the British soldiers in a crossfire.

* * *

As the gun battle erupted, Butler was struggling through dense undergrowth, anxious to join the fight. He stepped up the pace, not wanting to miss the battle. He was also concerned that Owens was out of his depth in a fight with the Germans. Butler had no idea that Donovan's team had arrived, so he was assuming that Owens, De Suter, and some of the miners were putting up a fight against the German spies.

As he ran, he tripped over what he thought was a log. He cursed as he tried to regain his footing. The log lifted its sleepy head and wrapped its enormous torso around Butler's left ankle, bringing him to an abrupt halt.

Butler had stumbled over a massive python. The beast was an African rock python. Almost six metres in length it was a common reptile in equatorial and sub-equatorial Africa. It fed on all manner of unsuspecting wildlife, including Butler, if it had its way.

While Butler struggled to free himself from the beast's death grip, the python reared its head and prepared to strike the partially immobilized soldier.

"Fuck, I guess Nash was right," he muttered to himself out of frustration, remembering his partner's paranoia at the ambush site the day before.

The massive beast struck at Butler, ripping its jaws into his left bicep. Butler grimaced in pain but had the sense of mind to reach into his boot with his right hand and pull out a large hunting knife. He twisted his torso to get a better angle of attack and sliced through the beast at the base of its skull, decapitating it. Blood spewed from the beast as it recoiled, convulsed, and finally went limp as death caught it up.

Butler shook the head of the dead reptile off his bicep and breathed a sigh of relief. He cut through the torso wrapped around his ankle and pulled his foot free of the python's corpse. Looking at the mammoth beast he whistled a sigh of relief and continued off in the direction of the gun fire, shaking his left arm which was now bleeding steadily.

* * *

Meantime, Donovan, McInerney and the two soldiers were trying, without success, to escape the crossfire. Meyer was well camouflaged, hidden by the jungle on one side of the truck. He was still positioned between Donovan's team and the train, while Fischer was hiding behind a log on the opposite side inside the gate, but a good distance from the office where Hofmayer was waiting to spring his trap. The Germans had locked the gate to prevent the Brits and Donovan getting into the compound.

Retreat would be their only option if they could not take down the Germans. Thankfully, the truck was providing cover and prevented the Nazis from gaining a direct line of fire. The Brits and Donovan kept the Germans' heads down with continuous fire, stopping them from getting behind the allied contingent.

"Watch your ammunition men," McInerney commanded, thinking the fight might take some time.

The four were armed with World War One vintage Lee-Enfield military-issue bolt-action rifles and Enfield Mk.1 revolvers. They were carrying a few hundred rounds of ammunition between them but no grenades or machine guns, which made the task of ridding themselves of the Germans more difficult.

The situation was made worse by the mine workers who had been loading the ore. Understandably, they were not interested in getting shot so had evacuated the loading area, retreating into the jungle as fast as their legs could carry them.

Back in the jungle, Butler was reconnoitering the situation trying to figure out the best way to attack the Nazis. He had wrapped a handkerchief around his bicep in an unsuccessful effort to stem the bleeding from the snake bite. He was surprised to see Donovan, McInerney and two soldiers at the scene of the battle. He could also see that Donovan's team was pinned down in a crossfire but putting up a good fight. The truck was under fire from the Germans on two sides, but from what he could tell from the limited gunfire, there were also only two Germans he needed to take care of.

He also knew from his encounter the day before there were three German agents, so the third must be somewhere close. He was hoping that no more had arrived since their ambush.

Meyer was nearest to him, about fifty metres in front of his position and concealed by the thick jungle, so Butler decided to attack that target first. He could hear the gun fire but could not make out where the German was hiding. Maneuvering to his left he looped around to what he thought would be Meyer's flank and narrowed the distance to about thirty metres. He also now had a better field of fire. He tossed a grenade towards the sound of the gunfire hoping to scare Meyer from his camouflaged position.

His plan worked. Meyer put his head up above the undergrowth and looked around to see who was throwing a grenade at him, which had landed and exploded harmlessly short of his position. He could not see his adversary, as Butler had crouched down and was also now hidden by the undergrowth. The German decided to move positions, assuming incorrectly, that he had been spotted. This proved to be a fatal mistake.

Now having a partial view of the German, who was running through the jungle towards the British truck, Butler took aim and fired, timing his shot to avoid trees providing cover to the soldier. He hit Meyer in the torso.

"Take that motherfucker," he muttered as Meyer collapsed in a heap. To make sure the German stayed down he put another round into him, but Meyer was dead before he hit the ground, the large caliber bullet ripping through his vital organs.

Fischer, seeing his senior officer go down, and now outgunned, made a run for it. He sprinted towards the relative safety of the mine office where Hofmayer was holed up. This was a mistake because he had to cover about fifty metres of open ground.

As soon as the German emerged from his covered position, Butler took aim through his high-powered scope and pulled the trigger. "Eat this, Kraut," he said aloud. Fischer collapsed to the ground as the bullet penetrated his neck and blew out his carotid artery, while also destroying his spinal cord. Butler got up and raced to the gate. He shot the lock off and joined Donovan's team as they entered the compound.

Donovan complemented the young officer, "Nice shooting commander. That is a nasty looking wound. Did you get shot?"

Butler shook his head and replied matter-of-factly, "Big snake. We better find Nash. I have a bad feeling about this," worrying far more about his friend than his flesh wound.

"That fat mother fucker is still out there somewhere," he told Donovan, referring to the third German agent.

The men did not have to wait long. Having seen his two underlings gunned down, Hofmayer came out of the office with Owens in tow, gagged, with his hands tied behind his back and a revolver pointed at his head. Butler and Donovan were in no doubt the German would not hesitate to pull the trigger.

"That is far enough," Hofmayer said aggressively to his adversaries. "If you want your friend to remain alive you will drop your weapons."

They were in a standoff.

"You are outnumbered, whoever you are," Donovan said, pointing out the obvious. "Drop your weapon and release our colleague. You cannot shoot all of us." The men spread out to make Hofmayer's task harder.

"I think not," Hofmayer said arrogantly as he held tightly onto his only bargaining chip. "Now drop your weapons!" he yelled, dictating his terms with venom, his pistol resting firmly on Owens' temple.

Donovan tried to stall, so he offered the Nazi a deal. "Let him go and you can take the truck and get out of here. No questions asked."

"No Mr. American. I am in control here and you will all drop your weapons immediately. I will take your friend and the train. If you try to stop me, I will kill your friend. Now, you have ten seconds to drop your weapons," he said with both a serious and confident look on his face. He cocked his pistol to reinforce the message that he was calling the shots.

Butler looked at Donovan, shifting his eyes to Hofmayer, indicating that he wanted to take a shot. Donovan shook his head. "Put down the guns, men," he said firmly to Butler and the soldiers. The men slowly dropped their weapons onto the ground.

"Now kick your weapons out of the way." Hofmayer ordered. The men complied and kicked their guns away from where they were standing.

Hofmayer, sensing victory, began dragging Owens towards the train. He knew that once he was on the train there would be little the Americans could do to stop him. The smile was violently wiped off his face seconds later, as the mine exploded a few hundred metres behind him. As instructed by De Suter, the workers let off the charges to seal the mine at precisely 1 p.m. Everyone, including Hofmayer and Owens, was knocked down by the massive concussion of the blast which also generated a heavy cloud of dust and dirt engulfing the camp and reducing visibility.

Butler regained his senses a few seconds ahead of Hofmayer. In the billowing dirt, soot and smoke, he crawled on his stomach to pick up his gun, stood up and yelled at Owens. "Move Nash!"

Owens rolled over, then again, distancing himself by a critical few feet from the German spy.

Hofmayer was as fast as Butler but losing his hold on Owens cost him the advantage. The German rolled over into a shooting position. He took aim and fired at Butler, just missing the American who was also ready to shoot.

Butler pulled the trigger a millisecond later, and before Hofmayer could get off a second round. He hit the Nazi spy in the forehead, the impact of the high-powered shell at close range splattering his skull and brains several feet in every direction.

He breathed a sigh of relief and raced over to Owens to make sure his friend was unharmed.

"Are you alright?" Butler asked Owens, helping his partner up, un-tying him and dusting him off.

"Fine," Owens replied. He was groggy and rubbed his jaw, feeling inside his mouth for loose teeth.

"You better check on De Suter. He is tied up in the office." Owens said to the men.

"Good work Dean," Donovan called to Butler, as they ran to the office to make sure De Suter was still alive.

"Are there any more of them?" Donovan asked Butler, wanting to be sure the enemy was no longer a threat.

"Not that I can see," Butler said with gun still firmly in hand.

"McInerney! Secure the area," Donovan commanded as he reached the office.

"Aye, Mr. Donovan," McInerney confirmed, as he and the healthy trooper checked the corpses and went about searching the area for more Germans.

Donovan freed De Suter and the two joined the group.

"Are you alright?" Donovan asked the Belgian.

"I am fine," De Suter said as he rubbed his rope burned hands.

"Good. Is the train ready to go?" Donovan asked, not wanting to delay the return journey any longer.

"Let me go up there and check on the situation, Mr. Donovan." De Suter headed off towards the train with the Americans following closely behind. Seeing that the situation was in hand the engineer and stoker nervously raised their heads above the guard rail of the engine. The engineer waved that he and his assistant were all right.

"That was good timing on the explosion Mr. De Suter," Owens said, complementing the Belgian.

"What is the American turn-of-phrase, Mr. Owens?" De Suter quipped managing a smile. "That it is better to be lucky than good?"

"You certainly couldn't have planned it any better, for sure," Butler agreed looking relieved. "And Nash?"

"Yes Dean?"

"You weren't so paranoid after all the other day," Butler winked, and showed off his wound.

"Who or what did that?" Owens asked Butler, making a face at the site of the wound.

"Big snake," again, was Butler's reply. Owens made another face and asked the engineer for a first aid kit which he duly threw to the diplomat, who tended to Butler's wound.

Donovan interrupted the small talk, satisfied that the train was ready to go. "Let's get going. Will you be all right here Mr. De Suter?"

"Yes. Once the ore is gone, and now the mine is sealed, there will be nothing left to take," De Suter said. "Can you leave us the radio from your truck? The Germans destroyed the telephone, and we will need a link to the outside world."

"Of course," Donovan replied.

"We will get the train back in a few days and load the heavy equipment onto flat cars. In a few months, the jungle will reclaim the mine," De Suter said with finality.

"Get your men to take the bodies into the jungle," Donovan instructed De Suter. "Let nature take its course. Officially we were never here."

"Consider it done," De Suter waved to some of his terrified laborers, who were slowly emerging from the jungle, to lend a hand.

McInerney and the healthy trooper joined the group.

"All is clear Mr. Donovan. There are no more of them." McInerney reported.

"Good."

"McInerney. Get your healthy soldier to ride the train with Butler and Owens. Hopefully, there are no more of them but another body on the train will be prudent, just in case."

"Ay, Mr. Donovan," McInerney said acknowledging the order and the healthy trooper jumped onto the train.

A smiling Dean Butler turned to his colleague. "Let's get going Nash. We have a train to catch." Owens and Butler jumped onto the engine joining the British soldier.

The engineer, looking relieved, said. "We should be back in time for dinner, and we will load the ship at first light."

Butler turned to Owens and said cheekily, "Nice going today, Nash. You are in the wrong line of work."

"Thanks. But a desk at State will do me fine," he said rubbing his badly bruised jaw and wiggling a tooth that would need work once he got back to Brussels.

CHAPTER TEN

PLOTTING AT THE PORT

L ate the next morning the American freighter Bobby Jean entered the port with the assistance of a tugboat. Goma was on hand to meet the ship and the uranium was sitting in rail cars ready to be loaded. Butler and Owens had supervised the delivery of the ore the night before and then returned to Leopoldville with the steam engine.

Standing at the gangplank Goma hailed the captain who was standing on deck. "Request permission to come aboard."

"Granted. Come on up." The Bobby Jean's captain called down to Goma. Goma walked up the gangplank and onto the main deck.

"Good morning, captain," Goma said. "I hope you had a safe passage. My name is Henri Goma. I am the port manager."

"Without incident thankfully," the captain said answering the first question. "My name is Steve Prentice. How long will it take to load the uranium Mr. Goma?"

"About twenty-four hours, give or take, and all going well. I expect you will be ready to depart late tomorrow. As you can see the ore is here, but it will take time to load as we only have one crane available to do the job, and it is loading another ship this morning," Goma replied, as he watched his stevedores load the ship birthed next to the Bobby Jean. There were still many pallets of freight on the dock waiting to be stowed.

"Ok. I do not want to be in port any longer than needed," Prentice said, knowing the risks involved in the operation.

"I have informed your American colleague Mr. Donovan of your arrival. He will brief you on the security situation. I recommend that you have an armed guard posted on the ship at all times."

"I will do so Mr. Goma," Prentice replied.

"Good. I will be in my office if you need anything," Goma said. "I would not advise that you or your crew leave the ship unless necessary. We can arrange supplies and fuel as required."

"Thanks. I will get a list of what we need and wait for Mr. Donovan," Prentice confirmed.

With the business concluded Goma returned to his office to continue his daily chores.

*　*　*

On the opposite side of the port, Ingrid Schuyler was standing on the deck of the Hildebrand plotting the demise of the American freighter. She was conferring with the ship's captain who was being dragged into the fight whether he liked it or not.

"It appears my colleagues failed in their mission captain," she said to Heitz, as they watched the activity on the opposite side of the port. "We have two choices. Either we sink the American freighter, or we board her and take control of the cargo," Schuyler said matter-of-factly, and somewhat naïvely. The Germans had things their own way on the continent, but the Belgian Congo was a long way from home and the Nazis had few military resources to call on if shooting broke out.

"If we take her, it will be an act of piracy and the Americans will be free to sink us when we leave port," Heitz replied, cautioning Schuyler against the second course of action.

Accepting her colleague's knowledge of maritime law, Schuyler shifted her focus to the first option. "Then we will sink her. There can be no consequences if there are no witnesses. Do you have diving gear on board?"

"Yes, Fräulein Schuyler," Heitz replied hesitantly, not wanting to involve himself or his crew in the spy's scheme.

"Good. I will arrange to have explosives delivered to the ship. Your job will be to plant them," she said, ignoring the captain's reluctant tone. "Can you manage that task?"

"Of course," the captain replied, knowing it was the only answer he could provide the devout Nazi. "When do you want us to plant the explosives?"

"Tonight, before they start loading the uranium." she replied, knowing that time was not on her side. "Once we dispose of the ship, we will use troops at the embassy to secure the port and load the uranium onto the Hildebrand. The Belgian authorities are weak and will not get in our way for fear of creating a diplomatic incident with the Führer."

"You will need to move the ship to that birth at the appropriate time." She pointed to the ship birthed beside the Bobby Jean which was still being loaded and would depart the port later that day.

With the plan in place, Schuyler left the freighter to sort out the explosives.

* * *

About an hour later, a British patrol boat arrived at the dock. McInerney was on the boat with the pilot and four soldiers. The launch pulled up alongside the Bobby Jean.

The boat was a CMB—Coastal Motorboat—built in 1915 to serve in the Great War. It had been retired after the war ended. The CMB was designed as an attack boat that could breach German defenses and sink much larger enemy vessels. Speed, stealth and agility were its best features. The boat could breach marine netting and avoid floating mines allowing it to attack enemy shipping in port.

She was solid teak and had been meticulously maintained since arriving in the Belgian Congo several years earlier, a gift from McInerney's predecessor who had it shipped from Cairo following his posting to Leopoldville. Since then, she had been serving as a vessel of leisure for the British embassy, spending her days cruising up and down the mighty Congo River, allowing embassy staff, their families, and guests to explore the inner country safely. McInerney was mindful that the CMB could be useful to the embassy for security operations, and had the boat retrofitted to carry a bow-mounted Vickers .303 machine gun. The CMB packed a punch and was finally about to serve the function that its designer had envisaged twenty-five years earlier.

"Ahoy captain," McInerney called to the bridge.

Captain Prentice leaned over the rail on the bridge. "Are you our security detail?"

"Affirmative captain," McInerney replied formally. "I am Lt. Colonel McInerney of His Majesty's marines. We have been instructed to provide all necessary assistance until you leave port."

"Very good Lt. Colonel. What do you recommend?" Prentice asked McInerney.

"I will post men on the dock and the boat will patrol the harbor until you depart," McInerney advised the captain.

"Thank you, Lt. Colonel. Carry on." Prentice replied.

Pointing at the four troopers, McInerney issued orders. "Boys, you are on shore patrol. You will be relieved at twenty-hundred hours." The troopers nodded and jumped off the boat. "You know the orders. Except for the port manager, our American friends, or our embassy staff, no one comes within fifty metres of the ship. Anyone trying to breach security shall be shot. Understood?"

The soldiers nodded their understanding but exchanged pensive looks. While the Congo was not a desirable post, it was also a quiet back water with little likelihood of action for green soldiers.

"Take me back to the port office and pick up the other marines," McInerney instructed the pilot. "Ensure no one, or any ship, comes close to the Bobby Jean mister. Do not,

I repeat do not, approach the German freighter. She is out of bounds."

"Aye, sir," the pilot said acknowledging McInerney's orders. He put the throttle down on the launch and it sped off in the direction of the port office.

* * *

The captain of the Hildebrand watched the British security detail through his binoculars. He did not like what he saw.

"Get the embassy on the radio," Heitz instructed his executive officer, a younger man named Schultz. "Get a message to Fräulein Schuyler. Tell her the American freighter is now being guarded by British troops. Also tell her there is an armed motor launch guarding access from the river. This will make it impossible to complete the mission she has in mind. Ask for instructions."

"Yes captain," Schultz replied, "right away."

Heitz quietly breathed a sigh of relief, hoping that neither he nor his men would be putting their lives at risk to rescue the mission.

* * *

Later that evening Owens and Butler drove around the perimeter of the port, following a rough dirt track that barely passed as a road. Both men had caught up on much needed sleep, only emerging from their rooms in time for dinner a few hours earlier.

An eight-foot-high fence topped with barbed wire separated the road from the docks. The fence was covered with vines and was there to prevent locals from stealing the valuable shipping cargo stacked on the docks. The plan called for Butler to use 808 explosives to disable or destroy the ship's propellers. 808, the plastic explosives of their time, were ignited by magnesium fuses, both of which were waterproof. If the plan worked the Hildebrand would be forced to remain in port to make repairs, while the Bobby Jean fled to New York with the uranium.

The quantity of explosives required was the variable that Butler and Owens were unsure of. Neither were experts, and the British embassy did not have an explosives' specialist on staff. It would be total guess work by Butler. While using too much 808 would accomplish the mission, it might also cause a large explosion and remove the element of surprise, putting Butler in danger both from the blast and discovery by the ship's crew.

It also risked putting a hole in the ship and sinking her. Donovan wanted to avoid this outcome as it would create another diplomatic incident, assuming of course that the Germans could prove the Americans were behind the skullduggery. Too little on the other hand, and the propellers might only suffer minor damage and be easily repaired.

The men had turned the truck's lights off to avoid being seen by the night watch on board the Hildebrand. They arrived outside the fence next to the ship and quickly got to work. Owens reversed the truck into the undergrowth of the jungle and covered it with a camouflage net.

Butler stripped down and put on a swimsuit. The river was warm so there was no need for a diving suit. He put on his diving gear which comprised a single tank with a hose, mouthpiece, regulator, and face mask. He carried his flippers and would put them on when he got into the river. He double checked the 808 and fuses which were stowed in a waterproofed canvas bag. It was almost twenty-two hundred hours.

"The lights should be going off in three minutes. Are you ready?" Owens asked Butler.

"As long as the 808 works, I am good to go," Butler replied confidently, patting the bag of explosives. "Do you have the bolt cutters?"

Owens held them up. "You need to be in and out in ten minutes," he reminded his partner for the third time.

"Roger Nash," Butler confirmed patiently. "Keep an eye on the Hildebrand. She is dark and looks quiet, but I am sure there are guards on deck somewhere. If I cannot get back here after I plant the explosives, I will meet you at the port office."

Both men took a final look at the Hildebrand but could not see anyone on deck. A minute later, Goma cut the lights at the port and turned on the air raid siren. The bleating noise of the siren shattered the silence of the quiet evening. The port was now pitch black. Goma locked the office as well as the access gate to the port, which would prevent the police from intruding on the mission. He went for a short walk to ensure he could not be found for the next little while.

"Ok. Let's go," Butler commanded Owens.

Owens pulled vines off a section of the fence and cut the wire, holding open the break while Butler slipped through. "Remember, ten minutes Dean," Owens repeated for the fourth time. Butler gave the thumbs up and crawled through the fence, slipping quietly into the water near the rear of the ship. He put on his flippers, mask and the tank, opened the valve on the tank to start the oxygen flow, took a breath and submerged.

Meanwhile, the Hildebrand's captain and executive officer came onto the main deck from the dining room, where they had been playing cards, trying to work out what was happening.

"I don't like this Schultz," Heitz said. "Open the weapons locker and arm the boys. Get them on deck to keep an eye out. If anyone approaches the ship, shoot to kill," he ordered coldly. "Fire up the generator and get some lights on."

"Yes captain." The executive officer disappeared from the deck to attend to his tasks. Heitz went quickly to his stateroom and took a Luger out of his desk drawer. The weapon was a standard issue German military handgun. He returned to the main deck to keep watch. The crew were emerging from the lower decks, armed and ready for action.

The backup generator kicked in and the Hildebrand lit up like a Christmas tree. A deck hand turned on a searchlight and began scanning the main channel in case they were attacked from the river. The British patrol boat was nowhere to be seen, having been ordered to stay well clear of the German freighter.

Butler was underwater attaching the charges to the screws of the freighter. By leaning against the stern of the ship, he was both too close to the hull to be lit up by the searchlight, and also invisible to the crew above. Talking to himself to stay calm, he gurgled. "Ok. Get this done."

Butler attached the charges to each screw, using a handful of explosives on each, hoping it would be enough to do the job. He then attached one magnesium fuse to each lump of the charge and broke each, which ignited the magnesium. The light from the ignited fuses was bright but somewhat muted by the murky river water.

Butler swam away from the ship and into the main harbor, deciding there were too many sailors on deck to allow him to safely go back the way he had come. Thankfully, the flames from the magnesium flares did not give Butler away. The charges were hidden by the ship's substructure, and ironically, the lights the captain had ordered be turned on.

But Butler did not have it all his own way. Unfortunately for the American, the searchlight lit him up as he retreated from the ship and a young seaman sounded the alarm. Butler submerged immediately to escape the beam.

A deck hand looked down at the illuminated harbor and saw carbon dioxide bubbles floating to the surface as Butler exhaled. Butler had made it about thirty metres into the channel. The seaman started shooting at the bubbles and called Schultz for help.

"Captain, there is someone in the water!" Schultz called from his position on the deck near the freighter's stern. "Keep the spotlight on the bubbles!" he yelled at the young sailor.

Heitz joined him at the stern and ordered his crew to fire at will. "There! Shoot there!" he called out pointing at the bubbles floating to the surface of the river.

Butler dove deeper and further away from the ship trying to escape the searchlight, but the Germans were now tracking the carbon dioxide he was exhaling. "Fuck!" he gurgled to himself as bullets hit the harbor all around him. He swam as fast as he could to put distance between himself and the ship, but the crew had him lined up. It was only a matter of time before they would find their mark.

Looking through his binoculars and pointing at the bubbles, Heitz yelled encouragement to his men.

"Whoever the intruder is, he will die," Heitz hissed under his breath to no one in particular.

One of the bullets hit Butler's tank and it started to leak oxygen. He decided it was time to change plan. He shook off the tank and pushed it away from his body. It promptly sank to the river bottom. He surfaced, took a deep breath, submerged again, and swam as fast as he could in the direction of the port office, which was at least a hundred metres away, holding his breath to shut off the carbon dioxide trail. He needed to get as far away as possible from the leaking oxygen tank which was drawing more fire from the Hildebrand's crew.

The Germans fell for the ruse. Pointing at the oxygen bubbling out of the tank the captain instructed the deck hands to focus on that single position. "Get the bastard. Follow the bubbles!" the captain yelled over the sound of the air raid siren. The sailors followed orders and kept firing.

Butler came up for a breath and checked his position in the water. He was now a good hundred metres from the Hildebrand and more importantly nowhere near the beam of the searchlight. Looking back at the German ship, he could see the deck hands firing on the spot where he had dropped the tank. The port office was still about seventy metres away but now he could take his time getting there as he was no longer in danger.

On the other side of the fence, Owens watched the Germans firing on what he also thought was Butler's position and decided he needed a diversion. He had no way of knowing his colleague was now out of danger. He grabbed a bag from the truck and ran along the fence line towards the bow of the Hildebrand.

Taking a grenade from his bag he pulled the pin and threw it over the fence and onto the dock. It exploded beside the Hildebrand causing no damage but diverting the attention of the merchant seamen.

Panicking, Schultz yelled at the captain, "We are being attacked from the jungle sir!"

Heitz replied without emotion, trying to stay calm, "I can see that. Get some of the men to return fire into the fence line."

He pointed in the general direction of Owens who was hiding in the undergrowth near the fence. "There can't be too many of the bastards."

Schultz fired wildly in Owens' direction while Owens threw another grenade and retreated further into the bush. The second grenade also exploded harmlessly on the dock but added to the confusion on the deck of the freighter.

A few seconds later a large bang sounded beneath the stern of the Hildebrand, and a huge spray of water erupted from the river soaking the deck. Instinctively the crew on station at the stern ducked for cover thinking they were being shelled.

The 808 had detonated and did its job leaving the propellers bent and mangled.

"What the fuck was that?" Heitz yelled to no one in particular, getting up after body slamming the deck to escape the explosion.

Together with a handful of his crew they looked down to the waterline to see what had happened.

Not only did the explosion incapacitate the Hildebrand, but it also diverted the attention of the Germans from Butler, who was almost at Goma's office. Owens also used the distraction to get out of the way. He got in the truck and retreated towards the port office to collect his partner.

The Hildebrand's captain and executive officer were trying to figure out what had happened. "What did you see?" Heitz asked a seaman who had been manning the stern.

"An explosion sir," the seaman said. "I do not know what it was. Perhaps a grenade?"

"I doubt it," Heitz said. "Did you get the diver?"

"The bubbles are gone sir. But I don't know if we hit the diver," the seaman replied honestly.

Another sailor pointed excitedly at Owens beating a retreat in the truck along the dirt track. "There sir!" the seaman called out, pointing his finger at the shadow of a truck bouncing along the track.

"Fire on that truck!" Heitz yelled, ordering his men to open fire. The captain had, had enough and was apoplectic. He wanted revenge and did not care how he got it. The sailors turned their guns on Owens who was still in range.

"Damn it," Owens cursed as bullets hit the truck, narrowly missing him. He ducked and hit the gas while zigzagging to evade the Germans bullets. The truck crashed through the bush, narrowly missing a large tree, as he put distance between himself and the crew of the Hildebrand.

Goma returned from his evening walk and turned the lights back on at the wharf. He also flipped the switch to shut off the irritating air raid siren.

"Very convenient," Heitz said to no one in particular.

"Get someone in the water Schultz. I expect we have been sabotaged."

"Aye sir," the executive officer acknowledged, his ears still ringing from the noise of the battle.

Butler climbed out of the water and onto the dock near the entrance to the port. He looked around to get his bearings. Seeing the port office, he walked calmly towards it. As he approached the office, he noticed a sign on the side of the building warning humans not to swim in the river due to the threat of crocodiles. He let out a slow whistle and thanked his good luck.

"Good evening Mr. Goma." He said calmly to the port manager as he walked into the office. "My name is Dean Butler; I work with Donovan."

"Good evening, Mr. Butler. Can I assist in any way?" Goma reciprocated, making small talk as if nothing had happened.

"Thanks, I am waiting for my ride. He should be here shortly," Butler said. "Can I borrow a towel?"

Goma opened a desk drawer, retrieved a towel, and threw it to Butler who began drying himself off after the long swim.

A truck drove into the compound at high speed and screeched to a halt. The Germans had shot out a rear taillight and put a hole in the spare tire during his retreat.

Aside from the minor damage, the truck and Owens were in one piece.

Owens was out of breath however, still not used to gun play.

"Let's make tracks Dean. It's a bit hot around here," Owens called out still full of adrenalin.

"Agreed. Good evening Mr. Goma," Butler said calmly. He got into the truck, and they drove off, passing a police car which had finally turned up to find out what the fuss was about.

Back on the bridge of the Hildebrand, the executive officer reported the damages to the captain. "They got the propellers sir. We will not be going anywhere until we repair them," Schultz said confirming Heitz's worse fears.

Heitz was calming down after the gun battle and quietly felt relieved, hoping that between the British security patrols and the damaged propellers, the Nazi spy might yet give up trying to get his crew killed.

"Get a message to the embassy. Tell Schuyler what happened," he ordered Schultz. "Get the machine shop fixing the propellers right way. I want to get out of this scheibloch as soon as they are repaired."

CHAPTER ELEVEN

LULL BEFORE
THE STORM

While the Americans and Brits were engaging the Germans in the jungle and on the water, on the diplomatic front a war of words was breaking out between the Nazis and the Brits.

Fräulein Schuyler had duly reported the predicament she was in to her bosses at military intelligence, and Admiral Canaris went to the Führer to report that Germany had competition from the Americans and British for the uranium. As a result, the Germans still had not taken possession of the resource.

It is fair to say he received a dressing down from the ill-tempered dictator.

Hitler was apoplectic, having already dealt with the humiliation of losing the Augustus to the Americans. He directed his ambassador to the United Kingdom, Eduard Willy Kurt Herbert von Dirksen, to rattle the cages at Whitehall, and drive a wedge between the two allies. He knew the Brits were weak and Chamberlain would melt if threatened, so he instructed von Dirksen to go full throttle, in diplomatic speak, on Lord Halifax the British Foreign Secretary.

Von Dirksen did as ordered and arranged a meeting with Halifax on the same evening that the Americans were sabotaging the Hildebrand.

Donovan and Creighton, however, were not 'born on a turnip truck' and had purposely left their political bosses in a position of deniability, so did not report the details of the gunfight the day before to Washington or London. Nor did they report their intention to sabotage the Hildebrand. Both were political veterans and knew when discretion was the better part of valor.

So as far as President Roosevelt and Prime Minister Chamberlain knew, aside from the confrontation with the German submarine, their teams had not encountered any issues repatriating the uranium and it would ship from Matadi in a matter of days.

Von Dirksen, meanwhile, arrived at Halifax's residence in Belgravia at 8 p.m. that same evening. He was afforded the usual diplomatic courtesies and shown into the foreign minister's drawing room. A formally attired butler offered the ambassador a beverage and he chose a nineteenth-century Spanish dry sherry. Lord Halifax appeared minutes later and joined von Dirksen for an aperitif.

After exchanging pleasantries, von Dirksen got to the point. "Lord Halifax, we have been getting some disturbing reports from our embassy in the Belgian Congo," he said, beginning the discussion politely.

Halifax, born with a poker face, replied, "that is unfortunate your excellency. Is there anything we can do to help?" He said disingenuously, fully knowing that he had an operation running in support of the Americans.

"We understand your government is providing aid to the United States government in a matter relating to an important mineral deposit," the ambassador started in an accusatory manner. "This deposit is subject to a jurisdictional dispute between the Reich, Belgium, and the United States."

Lord Halifax tried to downplay the situation. "Any assistance His Majesty's government may or may not be providing our American ally would only be logistical your excellency. I have not had any reports other than routine correspondence over the last few days," he said truthfully, while also not denying that the British were helping their American allies.

"Let me get to the point Lord Halifax," von Dirksen said more assertively. "We have reason to believe the Americans fired on one of our submarines recently, doing so with the full knowledge and support of your government."

"We also have evidence that the Americans, with the help of your government are actively, and illegally, attempting to take control of a mine that is legally owned by the Reich. The owner of the mine pledged its production to the Reich, and then reneged on that promise, creating a difficult legal predicament," he continued, substantially embellishing the truth to the British Foreign Minister.

While Sangier did promise to sell some of the mine's production to Germany, he had done so under duress. A fact Lord Halifax had been made aware of.

"I do not need to remind you and your Prime Minister that our countries are trying to work together to prevent an escalation of aggression in Western Europe," von Dirksen said menacingly, using typically twisted Nazi logic.

Lord Halifax mulled over the situation for a moment. While His Majesty's government was attempting to take a diplomatic approach to dealing with the mad German, it was becoming abundantly clear to Chamberlain and cabinet that they were being had. The Nazi invasion of Czechoslovakia was the slap in the face that finally forced the British Empire to awaken to the realities of dealing with the Nazi thugs.

Unfortunately, the Brits were in no position to pick a fight with Germany and had to be careful in its dealings with the much stronger, and aggressive, adversary. As a result, anything he said to von Dirksen would need to be communicated carefully.

To give himself a moment, he discretely signaled his butler to announce that his other engagement had arrived, to which the butler did promptly, knowing the game being played. "My apologies sirs. Your dinner engagement has arrived Lord Halifax," he said dutifully. In fact, once the German ambassador departed, Halifax would be enjoying a game of chess, over fish and chips and a bottle of 1936 Corton Charlemagne, with his trusted man servant.

Halifax apologized to von Dirksen and assured him he would raise the issue with the Prime Minister. "Mr.

Ambassador, please excuse me," he said standing. "I am afraid I have another engagement to attend."

Lord Halifax concluded the discussion by passing the buck. "I can assure you, Mr. Ambassador, that anything the Americans may be up to is a matter you need to take up with the United States government directly. And I would suggest that any legal issues between the two of you are properly taken up in a court of law."

"Having said that," he continued, throwing a carrot at the diplomat, knowing that von Dirksen would need to make a report to the Führer, "I am happy to contact our ambassador in the Belgian Congo, to make sure any assistance we are giving the Americans, if at all, will have no impact on your legal dispute."

The response gave the Brits a lot of leeway, and the ambassador a false assurance that the Americans were on their own.

"That would be most appreciated Lord Halifax," Von Dirksen said. "I will inform my Führer that our British colleagues will continue to adhere to the non-aggression agreements we have in place."

"This way Mr. Ambassador," the butler gestured, knowing Lord Halifax wanted out of the discussion. "I will show you out."

Von Dirksen was escorted to the front door of the townhouse. He had a commitment from the Brits that meant little. Nevertheless, he could now report to his Führer that the Brits would pose no threat as the competition for the uranium continued. The truth or not, his ass was covered.

* * *

Early the following morning Butler, Owens, and Donovan were at the hotel sitting at their now regular table in the garden having breakfast and enjoying the cooler morning air. Creighton arrived to join them. "Good morning, Creighton. What is the latest?" Donovan asked, greeting his SIS colleague.

Creighton sat down and poured himself a cup of tea. "You have a destroyer patrolling off the coast waiting to escort the freighter. Once she leaves port the three of you will be free to enjoy the sights," Creighton replied optimistically.

"Time to write some postcards," Donovan said humorously, although not totally convinced the Germans were going to give up just yet. He picked up his teaspoon and stirred his coffee as he considered the state of play.

Owens joined the discussion and confirmed what Donovan was thinking. "Maybe I am a worry wart, but what about our femme fatale? I very much doubt she will be sitting idly by and giving up without a fight. I presume also that the German embassy has enough troops at its disposal to cause us issues."

Both men's instincts were telling them that while the battles thus far had been won, the war in the Belgium Congo was far from over.

"We think Schuyler is holed up at the German embassy, but we haven't seen her," Creighton said updating the Americans on what he knew about the spy's whereabouts.

Butler also jumped into the discussion. "She does not have a lot of options. Once the freighter rendezvouses with the destroyer, even a sub won't tempt fate."

"So, we have today and potentially tomorrow morning to worry about, depending on how long it takes to load the uranium. Ideas?" Donovan said, opening the floor for discussion.

Butler got in first. "I would feel a lot better if I were on the launch with the Brits. That way I can keep an eye on the German freighter and be ready for any eventuality."

"Agreed," Donovan said. "Nash, why don't you keep an eye on the Hildebrand. That freighter is the most obvious platform for mounting an attack. Take a radio and stay out of sight."

"I will drop you off on the way Dean," Owens said, resigning himself to another jaunt in the jungle.

"Take me along. I will set up command on the Bobby Jean," Donovan said concluding that caution was the best policy at this stage of the mission. "Stay in touch Creighton," Donovan said to the SIS agent. "Radio me on the Bobby Jean if the woman turns up."

"I will do, Mr. Donovan," Creighton confirmed. With the plan settled, the men got up from the table to get ready for the day's work at the port of Matadi.

* * *

The Brits had not spotted Schuyler because she was on board the Hildebrand. Watching the uranium ore being loaded on the American freighter, the spy silently cursed her bosses for putting a dullard in charge of the operation. Had she been informed of the operation while in Lisbon, she would have taken care of the problem there, assuming correctly that the men she had met with Parker-Biggs were in fact leading the operation to extract the uranium. And as the American's had predicted, Schuyler was also not the type of spy to give up easily so was again plotting how to take or sink the Bobby Jean.

"What do you recommend captain?" Schuyler asked. The spy had slowly gained trust in the merchant seaman and his practical knowledge of all things maritime, so wanted his input before making a decision.

"We cannot board, or attack, her while she is at the berth. Not with all that security on the dock and the patrol boat in the river. Our only choice is to sink her," Heitz concluded after assessing the situation.

Agreeing with the captain's assessment of the tactical situation, Schuyler thought through the political, and career, impact of allowing the uranium to reach the Atlantic.

"The Führer will not be happy if the uranium reaches the United States. And by that, I mean that all those involved in a failure of the mission will be held to account." The spy concluded fatalistically. While she had her scape goat in Hofmayer, she did not want to risk being tarred with the same brush of failure.

Heitz tried to be helpful, while also hoping he was not on Schuyler's failure ledger. "She will be weighing heavy when she leaves port Fräulein Schuyler. She will need the tugboat to navigate the river channel and get her out to sea," the captain explained.

"What are you suggesting captain?" Schuyler said not quite following.

"Our best chance will be to attack her when she is under tow." He explained methodically. "She will be running heavy and doing less than five knots so she will be an easy target. We have a motor launch on board. We can pack it with explosives and run the launch into the freighter," Heitz explained, reluctantly laying out his plan, knowing that in all likelihood he would be the 'volunteer' piloting the launch.

"Yes, that will work," Schuyler agreed enthusiastically. "We already have the mines on board. I will get more explosives from the arsenal at the embassy. When do you think the Americans will get underway?"

"They look to be about halfway through loading the ore," he said as he watched, through his binoculars, the crane loading the Bobby Jean. "I would estimate the freighter leaving port later this afternoon or early this evening."

"Good. I will be back in a few hours."

The German spy strode purposefully down the gangplank and got into a Mercedes. She was pleased knowing she had a plan that might work.

Owens had arrived a few minutes earlier and taken up position in the jungle outside the fence, close to where he had been the previous evening. Thankfully, there was other traffic using the road around the port that day, so he managed to blend into the local scenery and avoid discovery by the Hildebrand's look out. He saw Schuyler leave the German freighter and immediately called Donovan. "Come in Bobby Jean. This is Owens."

"This is the Bobby Jean. Is this Mr. Owens?" the radio operator asked.

"It is. Donovan please."

"Stand by," the radio operator said.

"Donovan here."

"It is Nash, Bill. Our female friend is leaving the Hildebrand," Owens reported.

"Thanks Nash. Stay with the Hildebrand and let me know if she comes back," Donovan ordered.

"Yes sir." Owens acknowledged, pleased he had found the key remaining player.

On the Bobby Jean, Donovan turned to Captain Prentice and asked. "Can you get a message to Creighton at the British embassy and let him know that the spy just left the German freighter. Tell him to report back if she returns to the embassy."

"Consider it done," Prentice replied, and instructed the radio operator to do the needful.

* * *

Butler was on the CMB patrolling the harbor near the American freighter. He climbed on deck from the small compartment below where he had been catching up on lost sleep. The activities of the last two days were taking their toll on the young officer.

McInerney's second in charge at the embassy, Captain Henderson, had taken over responsibility for the CMB. Henderson handed Butler a cup of tea.

Like McInerney, Henderson was a career officer on the embassy circuit. In his early thirties, he was a slight man, standing five foot six inches, and 130 pounds. He was dressed in desert gear, wearing a short sleeve shirt, shorts and long socks. He had grown up in the Channel Islands, the British controlled archipelago just off the coast of France, and as such was a mad, keen sailor and very much at home on the motor launch.

"Thanks captain. Anything new?" Butler asked.

"All quiet, Lieutenant Commander. Did you get any sleep?" the captain asked politely.

"Enough to keep me going. I expect it will be a long day," Butler replied. "Swing her around to the opposite side of the wharf. Let the Germans know we are here."

"Aye Lieutenant Commander," Captain Henderson said acknowledging the order. Despite outranking the young officer, Henderson would take orders from the American on this mission. The helmsman put the throttle down and the CMB sped effortlessly across the river towards the Hildebrand.

Owens was still hiding in the jungle watching the German freighter. A truck drove up and started unloading supplies. Owens picked up the transmitter and raised the Bobby Jean.

The radio operator passed him on to Donovan who was drinking coffee and eating a sandwich. "Donovan here. What is the latest Nash?"

"There is a truck unloading supplies onto the Hildebrand, Bill. I cannot tell what the cargo is, but all the wooden crates look to be identical," Owens reported.

"Given the ship isn't going anywhere soon that can't be good," Donovan concluded.

"They have had divers working underwater all day, Bill. Maybe they have repaired the screws and are getting ready to leave." Owens suggested.

"Maybe, but I doubt it," Donovan replied. "She can't do any damage if she leaves port. Update me as required Nash."

"Yes sir," Owens signed off.

* * *

On the Hildebrand, deck hands were loading the wooden crates onto the launch on the port side of the ship, out of Owen's view. "There is enough dynamite on board to blow up the port, captain," Executive Officer Schultz observed, looking at the considerable number of crates, all packed with explosives, piled on the deck waiting to load onto the launch.

"We only have one chance and if we miss, you and I won't have much of a future in the Reich," the captain conceded knowing they would be in a lose-lose situation if they failed. "Leave some crates behind just in case." Heitz wanted an insurance policy in the unlikely event that ramming and blowing up the American freighter failed.

"Who is going to pilot the launch captain?" Schultz asked nervously, not really wanting to know the answer.

"You and I are the volunteers," Heitz replied stoically. "We will aim the launch at the American freighter, tie down the wheel, jump for our lives and hope for the best."

At that moment, Schuyler arrived on deck. "All is set?"

"We need to attach the fuses to the timer to complete the wiring. When would you like us to attack the Americans?" Heitz asked without enthusiasm knowing there was a better than even chance he and his executive officer would be blown to bits that afternoon.

"When the freighter gets ready to depart the dock," Schuyler ordered. "Our only opposition will be the British launch and I will take care of that problem."

"How do you plan to do that Fräulein Schuyler?" The captain asked.

"Leave that to me. Drop the launch into the harbor when the tugboat is ready to tow the American freighter. I want to give them as little time as possible to mount a defence."

"Yes, Fräulein. We will be ready," Heitz confirmed.

"You will be heroes of the Fatherland gentlemen," she said forcing a smile. Schuyler was doing her best to build their confidence, but knew they were merchant seaman with no military training. But they could not do any worse than the incompetent Hofmayer, she thought to herself. She presumed Hofmayer and the two soldiers had been killed by the Americans as they had not contacted her, or the embassy, in the last two days. Schuyler left the Hildebrand and drove back to the German embassy to prepare for her own mission later that afternoon. The two sailors looked at each other pensively, not convinced they would come out of this mess as heroes.

Owens watched Schuyler board the freighter, and then depart fifteen minutes later. He radioed the update to Donovan. "Our female friend came and went, Bill. She did not stay long," Owens reported.

"Okay. Pack up Nash. I need you with me. Butler and his crew are going to watch the Hildebrand from the launch," Donovan ordered.

"Roger Bill. On my way," Owens packed up the radio and scrambled back through the bush to his truck.

* * *

A truck pulled up next to the Bobby Jean a half hour later. Creighton and Parker-Biggs got out. "Permission to come aboard. Creighton and Parker-Biggs from His

Majesty's government reporting for duty." The local MI-6 agent announced melodramatically.

"Go aboard sirs," the young soldier manning the gangplank replied, recognizing Creighton and moving aside, allowing the men onto the freighter.

"Good afternoon old boy," Biggs called enthusiastically to Owens.

"Parker-Biggs. What brings you to the colonies?" Owens replied looking both pleased and surprised as the Brits appeared on the bridge.

"The Foreign Office decided you could use some help," Biggs announced with his usual tone of understatement.

"I hope you brought your crystal ball. We have no idea what the Nazis are planning," Owens confessed.

"There has been a lot of action on the Hildebrand this morning, Peter," Donovan said to Creighton as he joined the discussion. "Our favorite spy has been visiting and they have been loading cargo."

"That can't be good," Creighton replied with concern.

"Where is your colleague, Butler?" Biggs asked.

"On the harbor," Owens replied passing the binoculars to Biggs.

"If nothing else, I expect when the shooting starts, the Lieutenant Commander will be in the thick of it," Biggs theorized as he watched the CMB patrol the harbour. Biggs knew the American naval officer was the gung-ho type and would go looking for trouble if the opportunity arose.

"I expect so," Donovan agreed.

"How can we help?" Creighton asked.

"Find out what the woman is up to. She is the key to this," Donovan directed the MI-6 men, and confirming what all were thinking.

"We will take over watch at the German embassy. There is nothing we can do while she is on German soil. But we will follow her if she leaves," Creighton replied, assuming that would be the most likely location for the spy to be hiding.

"By the way, Bill. The ambassador popped into my office this morning. The Germans are rattling the cages politically. The German ambassador met with Halifax last evening, threatening the 'peace' if we continue to give assistance to the Americans on this mission."

"What did Halifax tell him?" Donovan asked, not at all surprised the Nazis were pulling out all stops to get the uranium.

"That he would take the matter under advisement," Creighton replied. "Which means doing nothing. It seems the politicians are finally waking up to the realities of dealing with the Nazis."

"Good." Donovan said, "take a radio and report her every movement."

"Off we go Biggs. Let me show you the sights of Leopoldville," Creighton said jokingly, trying to defuse the tension on the bridge.

"I am sure it is a charming town," Biggs replied with a wink.

"Leave her to us Bill. I will ring you on the wireless when we have something meaningful to report," Creighton said.

"Very good. Later gentlemen," Donovan replied sending the British spies on their way back to Leopoldville.

"And make sure you carry weapons," he called after the men as they disembarked the freighter.

It was mid afternoon by the time Creighton and Parker-Biggs returned to Leopoldville and relieved the two British soldiers who had been watching the embassy. The soldiers reported that Schuyler had returned to the embassy earlier that afternoon. They parked across the street, and sat down at a nearby roadside bar, enabling them to watch the embassy without being seen. There were very few white faces on the streets of Leopoldville, so the men hid behind menus and newspapers.

A black Mercedes sedan came out of the embassy about an hour later. Schuyler was in the back seat with two uniformed soldiers in the front. "Follow that car, as they say," Biggs said to his SIS colleague. Creighton left ten francs on the table, and gave the Germans a head start. The Brits followed Schuyler at a discrete distance.

"They are heading north, away from the port," Creighton announced quizzically to Biggs, wondering why the spy was going in the wrong direction.

* * *

It was late afternoon; the ore was loaded, and the Bobby Jean would be ready to sail as soon as the stevedores finished filling her tanks with diesel. A tugboat was alongside rigging the freighter for towing. "We will be ready to get underway in about thirty minutes Bill. Do you want to get off here or catch a ride back with Butler once we get further downstream?"

"We will hang around captain," Donovan decided. "Whatever the Germans are up to they will show their cards soon. Get Butler on the radio please captain?"

"Aye Mr. Donovan," Prentice said to the radio operator. "Get the patrol boat on the horn."

The radio operator passed the handset to Donovan.

On the patrol boat, a sailor handed the microphone to Butler. "It is for you sir."

"Yes Bill?"

"We are almost ready to get underway Dean. What are the Germans up to?" Donovan asked.

"Last we checked all was quiet. Do you want us to run over and have a look?"

"No. Stay off our starboard side, about a hundred metres. If anything comes your way intercept it," Donovan said issuing the command.

"Shoot first sir?" Butler asked, seeking clarification of the rules of engagement.

"Affirmative," Donovan replied.

"Roger," Butler confirmed signing off.

"Safeties are off Captain Henderson," Butler announced to the British commander, confirming the shoot first policy.

"Ay, Lieutenant Commander." Henderson acknowledged.

Butler picked up his binoculars and scanned the harbor. Like his colleagues on the freighter, he was wondering what the Germans were up to.

CHAPTER 12

COUNTERATTACK

N orth of the port, at a fishing village on the Atlantic
Ocean, Schuyler and the two soldiers from the
embassy stopped at the pier. They approached the captain
of a large fishing boat. He was sitting on the beach mending
his nets from the day's fishing.

"Is this your boat?" Schuyler asked the fisherman,
pointing at the forty-foot launch tied up to the pier.

"Yes, she is mine," the fisherman replied suspiciously.
Caucasians were not common in the local fishing
community.

Schuyler pulled out a roll of francs from her pocket.
"We need to rent it for a couple hours."

Looking at the Germans, and deciding he would
be no match for them, particularly the fearsome looking
woman, the fisherman took the money. "Bring her back in

one piece," he said, wondering if he would ever see his boat again.

A quick count of the francs soothed his fears. Schuyler had given him enough money to buy a new boat.

"Let's get going," Schuyler said to her two henchmen. They grabbed two bags of equipment, boarded the vessel, and sped off towards Matadi, the big diesel engine pushing out more than enough power to get the German's to their destination in plenty of time.

Parked across the road from the pier, the SIS men had observed the transaction. Creighton put the headset on and radioed the American freighter.

"Come in Bobby Jean," Creighton called. "Repeat. Come in Bobby Jean." The line was staticky as they were about fifteen kilometres north of the American freighter.

"Bobby Jean here. Standby," the radio operator said picking up the transmission on the agreed frequency.

"Is that you Creighton?" Donovan asked, taking over from the radio operator.

"Yes Bill," Creighton responded through the static. "The Germans have taken a fishing boat about fifteen kilometres north of you and are heading your way."

"We will keep an eye out for it. Game on Mr. Creighton," Donovan concluded, a mix of anxiety and excitement building in his voice.

"God speed Mr. Donovan. Out." Creighton said signing off.

"Trouble?" Parker-Biggs asked.

"So, it appears. We had better get back to Matadi."

Creighton turned the truck around and hit the gas. They had a fight to get to.

* * *

Donovan, Prentice, and Owens were on the bridge discussing the situation knowing the fishing boat would probably be running interference for the Hildebrand. A lookout on the Bobby Jean watched a large motor launch move slowly away from the Hildebrand. The sailor came onto the bridge and reported the enemy activity.

The men immediately turned their attention to the German launch.

"Has your marksmanship improved Nash?" Donovan asked seriously.

"Not really," Owens replied shaking his head.

"Break out arms Mr. Prentice," Donovan ordered. "If that motor launch or the fishing boat get in our way start shooting. Where are you meeting the destroyer?"

"About ten kilometres out," Prentice said.

"Tell her to get within firing range and standby. We might need her big guns. Also let Butler know that we have another target approaching," Donovan said taking charge of the situation.

* * *

The crew of the CMB had been watching the launch leave the side of the Hildebrand. Butler had De Suter's hunting rifle out and was targeting the boat through the scope.

"Sir. A message from the Bobby Jean," the radio operator called out to Butler over the noise of the engines. "We have another target inbound. A fishing boat with three

Germans on board including the spy. Should be entering the channel shortly."

"Roger. Captain, keep us between the Germans and the Bobby Jean. If that launch moves towards our freighter, open fire," Butler ordered, pointing at the German launch as it slowly moved into the main channel and away from the Hildebrand.

"Aye, aye sir. Battle stations men," the captain ordered. The crew broke out small arms and stood by. The machine gun crew on the bow loaded the Vickers and sent a test burst into the river.

* * *

It didn't take Schuyler and her soldiers long to reach the mouth of the Congo and the fishing boat was making its way up the river approaching Matadi. Schuyler watched the plan unfold through her binoculars.

"Head towards that launch," Schuyler ordered her colleague, pointing at the CMB several hundred metres in the distance. "Get me into shooting range."

"Yes Fräulein," the German crewman replied. He pointed the big fishing boat towards the British launch and pushed down the throttles. Schuyler unpacked her high-powered rifle from its case and assembled it. Like the rifle that Butler borrowed from De Suter, Schuyler's rifle shot large, high caliber bullets designed to bring down elephants. It would do considerable damage if she found her mark.

She opened the second bag which contained a Mauser infantry rifle and a prototype of a new German infantry weapon. Called the Schiessbecher, the weapon was a first-generation grenade launcher designed to be fired from the Mauser. The gun was currently being evaluated by the Wehrmacht and she was intent on putting it to good use. She loaded a grenade onto the end of the rifle. She was ready to do battle.

* * *

Butler was watching the Hildebrand's motor launch as it began to steer towards the American freighter. At the same time, a soldier on the CMB spotted the fishing boat cruising at speed towards them.

"Civilian vessel off our bow Lieutenant Commander Butler. Bearing due west in the middle of the channel," the crewman said pointing at the boat making its way up the main channel of the Congo River.

"Steady as she goes captain," Butler commanded as he thought through the best strategy of dealing with two enemy vessels. "Keep us between the Hildebrand's launch and the Bobby Jean," he ordered, deciding the more important objective was preventing the launch from attacking the American freighter. It would mean taking punishment from Schuyler on the fishing boat, but they had no other choice. He had to pick the poison most likely to damage or disrupt the Bobby Jean.

"Yes sir," the captain confirmed as he kept the patrol boat in position.

On board the Hildebrand's launch the captain and executive officer were maneuvering their boat towards the Bobby Jean. "Set the fuses and timer Schultz. Give us five minutes," Heitz ordered.

The executive officer went about his task as directed. "Explosives set for five minutes," he confirmed a minute later.

Heitz was also watching the action unfold through his binoculars. "Looks as if Fräulein Schuyler is going to run interference," he said pointing in the direction of the fishing boat about two hundred metres off his starboard side. "I am going to full speed. Jump off on my signal." He ordered Schultz as he took the launch to full speed.

Butler watched as the Hildebrand's launch went full throttle and sped towards the Bobby Jean with deadly intent.

"Close the distance and open fire on that launch captain," Butler commanded as the action heated up. The British crew and Butler opened fire on the explosive-laden motor launch. The machine gun crew raked the water around the launch but had not yet found the range of its adversary.

On the fishing boat Schuyler had her high-powered rifle centred on the British patrol boat. "Hold her steady," Schuyler yelled to the soldier piloting the vessel. She took aim at the CMB and opened fire. In total she put six slugs into its side forcing the Brits to take evasive action. Her seventh exploded through the left shoulder of a young soldier who crumpled to the deck in pain. Schuyler was on point and kept the sailors' heads down, making it difficult for them from firing on the Hildebrand's launch.

Captain Henderson was also struggling to keep the CMB between the explosive-packed German launch and the American freighter, as he was forced to steer in a zigzag pattern to evade Schuyler's deadly fire.

On the Hildebrand's launch, Heitz and his executive officer had the boat in position to collide with the Bobby Jean. Thanks to Schuyler's efforts they were making an almost unimpeded run at the American freighter.

"Tie down the wheel, then abandon ship!" Heitz yelled at Schultz. "We are as close as we can get."

"Aye captain. Ready when you are," Schultz replied as he tied the wheel in position.

"Now!" Heitz yelled. Both men leaped off the launch and into the Congo River, hitting the water violently.

Butler and the captain watched as the Germans abandon ship, then ducked for cover as a bullet hammered the side of the launch taking another sizeable chunk of teak out of her side.

"We need to intercept that launch before it hits the Bobby Jean!" Butler yelled as he crouched down on the deck. The captain needed no instruction. He pushed the CMB to full speed and steered straight towards the enemy launch.

"Keep it up boys!" the captain yelled, encouraging his men to ignore the incoming fire, as he maneuvered the CMB to intercept the launch. "Get some fire on that fishing boat before it sinks us!"

As if on cue, there was an explosion about ten metres off the CMB's stern. Schuyler had changed tactics and let loose with the grenade launcher. If it found its mark the result would be deadly.

On board the Bobby Jean, Bill Donovan and Nash Owens watched the drama unfold. The German motor launch was speeding straight for the starboard side of their ship, while the CMB was trying to cut it off. The Bobby

Jean's crew were putting fire on the fishing boat but not slowing Schuyler down. Unfortunately, the Americans were powerless to defend the freighter, reduced to being spectators as they watched the deadly spectacle unfold. Small weapons fire from the Bobby Jean's crew would have no effect on the outcome of the battle.

"Evacuate the ship captain," Donovan ordered. "Get everyone off except essential personnel."

Prentice issued the order over the loudspeaker and the crew, with the exception of the sailors on the bridge, as well as Donovan and Owens, beat a hasty retreat down the gangplank and well clear of the freighter.

The fishing boat continued to have its way with the CMB. However, the British vessel was made of solid teak and could withstand the force of the bullets exploding into her hull. A direct hit from the spy's grenade launcher would be a different story, however.

"Get the destroyer on the line, captain," Donovan ordered, deciding it was time to bring in the big guns into play.

"Bobby Jean to USS Charlotte. Come in Charlotte," the captain said as he took charge of the radio.

"This is the Charlotte. Go ahead Bobby Jean," the radio operator on the Charlotte replied.

Donovan took the handset from the captain. "This is Bill Donovan. Put the captain on."

"Hold sir." There was a pause as the operator gave the handset to the captain.

"This is Captain Billingsley. What do you need Mr. Donovan? We have just arrived on station and can provide any support you need," he reported.

"We are under fire captain and need some assistance."

"We are ready and waiting Mr. Donovan. Knox briefed us personally. What do you need?"

"We have two ships trying to intercept our cargo. There is a fishing vessel firing on our launch. It is about five kilometres east or your position. Can you see it?"

"We have it in sight."

"Sink it captain," Donovan said with authority. "We will look after the other one."

The Charlotte went to battle stations and Billingsley ordered his gunnery to start shelling the fishing boat, which was continuing to lob grenades at the British patrol boat.

The first shell from the destroyer landed fifty metres short but got Schuyler's attention. "Get us closer!" she yelled, ordering the fishing boat to close the distance with the CMB.

"Yes Fräulein," the German crewman replied with a distressed look on his face, as he could see the American destroyer in the distance. While he was regular army, he had never been to war and was naturally terrified at the prospect of the destroyer blowing the fishing boat out from underneath him. "We cannot stay much longer. The destroyer will have us in range in a minute," he warned the steely nerved spy.

"The Fatherland is more important. Do as I order," Schuyler scowled ignoring the young soldier. She reloaded the grenade launcher and ordered the second crewman to fire on the CMB with her high-powered rifle. The helmsman turned the fishing boat and closed the distance with the CMB.

But she was too late to intercept the Brits, as Captain Henderson had the patrol boat almost alongside the Hildebrand's launch. Both vessels were now running a parallel course heading straight for the Bobby Jean.

Butler looked inside the launch. "It is loaded with explosives! How much time have we got before it hits the Bobby Jean?"

"Less than a minute Lieutenant Commander. What do you want to do?" the captain said, trying to stay calm but knowing time was running out.

"Help me board her captain, then get out of the way," Butler said calmly. The captain steered the CMB within a metre of the German launch. Butler handed his rifle to one of the marines and leaped onto the German launch, landing on the explosives.

"Shit," he said to no one in particular, holding his breath and expecting the worse.

Thankfully, Butler's weight did not trigger an explosion, but he could see the timer running down. There were about 30 seconds left before he and the Bobby Jean, including Donovan and Owens, would be blown to bits.

He looked quickly at the dynamite and saw the explosives were wired and attached to a single timer. He only had seconds to decide how to disarm the dynamite. However, he did not know if pulling the fuse wires out of the timer would trigger an explosion. "Fuck," he said to himself knowing it was do or die time.

Looking up he could see the launch was only about forty metres from the Bobby Jean. He then looked at the timer which was under twenty seconds.

He made his decision and decided to leave the explosives alone. He took the hunting knife out of his boot and cut the rope holding the steering wheel in place. While the knife was sharp it still took valuable seconds to cut the rope, and the launch was now staring down the Bobby Jean.

Taking control of the wheel Butler executed an aggressive turn, showering the American freighter with the wake as the launch was barely ten metres from the Bobby Jean. He pointed the German boat down the channel in the direction of the fishing boat. The timer on the explosives had almost run out as he abandoned ship. He landed violently in the harbor, the river feeling like a brick at high speed. The German launch ran straight and true and a few seconds later exploded in the middle of the harbor sending debris flying everywhere.

Schuyler witnessed the explosion in front of her and immediately ordered the fishing boat to take aim at the Bobby Jean. She was not giving up despite a shell landing ten metres off the starboard side of the fishing boat, engulfing the vessel with water. Schuyler and the German soldiers were now taking fire from two directions, but she was about to get help in the form of U-073.

* * *

While the Germans had thrown everything into the plan to disrupt, destroy, buy, or steal the uranium, they had failed to achieve any of their goals. The Führer's vision of creating a massive bomb powered by Belgian Congo uranium was not looking hopeful, thanks to the efforts of Donovan, Owens, and Butler as well as their British colleagues.

Diplomatic efforts by the Germans to bully their British and American counterparts had also fallen on deaf ears. Both the United States and Britain knew that, on the eve of the second world war, the uranium from the mine in Shinkolobwe would eventually give the Allies a strategic advantage over their foes. More importantly, they new that Hitler would be able to dictate the terms of a new world order if the Nazis gained control of the resource.

But just as Donovan thought that the Nazis had played their final card with the destruction of the German launch, another player re-joined the table—U-073. The submarine, having missed the opportunity to take the Augustus and its cargo, was despatched to the west coast of the Congo. Her orders were to sink any naval escorts and hijack or, in the worse case, sink the Bobby Jean and its cargo.

Captain Jaanzen had briefed his crew two days earlier and while none were looking forward to another scrap with an American destroyer, they were resolute to do their duty. Donitz and Canaris had made it clear that the uranium was to be despatched to the bottom of the Atlantic if there was no possibility of hijacking the American freighter.

U-073 was cruising just under periscope depth several kilometres north of the Charlotte. The sonar operator called Executive Officer Schneider to his station. "We have a stationary contact about ten kilometres south," he reported.

Schneider looked for himself. Seeing the blip on the screen, he went to the desk where Jaanzen was eating an apple and going over his charts.

"We have a stationary target captain, about ten kilometres, 172 degrees," Schneider reported.

"Thanks," Jaanzen replied coolly. "Go to periscope depth."

A few minutes later the captain spun the periscope around to get a 360-degree view. His eyes settled on an American destroyer that was likely waiting for a cargo ship to join it in the Atlantic. The destroyer was also unloading on a target up the Congo River. Smoke plumes were exiting its forward gun with regular frequency.

The target was beyond maximum range for the submarine's new generation G7E torpedoes, so the captain ordered the helmsman to close the distance. The torpedoes could do considerable damage with their 300-kilogram warhead, but testing found the new weapon to be unreliable. The magnetic contact pin was prone to failure, and this combined with its limited range and slow speed, made the process of mounting an attack on anything other than a defenceless merchant ship, a nerve-wracking experience for sub crews.

The captain whistled nervously and announced to the crew on the bridge that they were about to do battle, "The contact is an American destroyer. She is firing on someone or something." He reported as he watched the destroyer's forward guns continuing to fire shells inland.

"Have a look at our target Schneider," Jaanzen said as he moved aside to let his executive officer view their target.

"Orders, sir?" asked Schneider, as he stared at the destroyer, knowing the likely answer to his question.

"Battle stations!" the captain announced sounding the alarm. "Load the four forward tubes. Fire in a ten second spread on my order."

"Tell me when we are within firing range Schneider." Jaanzen ordered, referring to the torpedoes' five-kilometre range.

The tension on the bridge was thick. The crew knew that if they failed with their first attack, they probably would not get a second opportunity. But they had a stationery target, and that factor alone made the captain's decision to attack much easier.

The sub continued to close distance with the destroyer, and the captain patiently waited for Schneider's confirmation that they were within five kilometres of their target.

"In range captain." Schneider said finally. To narrow the odds of a hit, he had waited until the sub was 4,500 metres from the destroyer.

"Fire one, fire two, fire three, fire four," Jaanzen ordered at ten second intervals. The torpedo room sailor pulled the release levers precisely on the captain's order and the fish were away. There was nothing to do but wait. "Take us to fifty metres, helmsman." Jaanzen ordered.

Schneider started his stopwatch to time the attack.

"All engines stop," the captain ordered as the sub reached her depth. He needed at least one of the torpedoes to find its mark. If the torpedoes missed, then they would play possum and hope the destroyer would not find her. They could not outrun the destroyer so they would try to out fox her.

The entire crew stood silently and waited for the sound of an explosion.

*　*　*

The Bobby Jean was in range of the grenade launcher, so Schuyler took aim and fired the Mauser. Her plan was to takeout the bridge, including the captain and the American spies. She scored a hit on her first attempt, but the grenade was a dud and bounced harmlessly off the starboard side of the freighter.

"Sheisse," she cursed to herself. The grenade launcher was a difficult weapon to use on an unstable platform like the fishing boat, which was bouncing around in the river, but she had nevertheless overcome the challenge, only to be let down by the explosive.

The crew of the Bobby Jean was helpless and nothing more than a bystander as the next round of the battle got underway. The CMB was busy plucking Butler out of the river. Schuyler's fishing boat was out of range for the Bobby Jean's crew who were now returning to the ship. The sailors only had small arms at their disposal. But they were in range of the German spy, and her grenade launcher, and this was the advantage the Abwehr agent fully intended to exploit.

"Hold her steady," Schuyler ordered the helmsman. She loaded the grenade launcher for another round and took aim at the Bobby Jean's bridge. The boat hit a wave as she pulled the trigger on the Mauser, and the grenade missed its mark, exploding in the river ten metres from the American freighter. The German helmsman immediately did a zigzag expecting another shell from the destroyer, but there was nothing inbound. The Charlotte had her own problems.

* * *

"Torpedoes captain!" a lookout yelled from the forward deck. The sailor pointed in the direction of the inbound threats, cruising towards the destroyer, less than three hundred metres away.

Grabbing his binoculars and seeing a four 'fish' spread aimed squarely at the starboard side of the destroyer, Billingsley yelled battle stations and ordered evasive action. The alarm sounded and the ship's crew sprang into action.

"Ahead full, forty-five degrees to bow helmsman. Point the ship at the torpedoes," Billingsley ordered calmly. The crew of the Charlotte had trained to combat this threat and their professionalism under fire would now be put to the test.

The helmsman pushed the big destroyer into gear, and it lurched forward, turning into the threat to narrow its target radius. The first torpedo comfortably missed the starboard side of the destroyer, but the second would be close. The crew held its collective breath as the second fish missed the destroyer by less than a metre.

"Hard to starboard mister," the captain ordered as the ship rapidly gained speed. The destroyer made an aggressive right turn just in time to miss the third torpedo. Ten seconds later the final torpedo missed well wide of its mark.

"Find that sub!" Billingsley ordered his team. They had just survived forty seconds of terror and the captain's mission was now to find and destroy the submarine.

"And radio the freighter. Tell them they are on their own."

* * *

The CMB had turned around and fished Butler out of the river, while Schuyler continued her assault on the American freighter. Throwing a towel to Butler, the captain smiled at the American sailor who was now safely back aboard albeit with a nasty headache from the concussive effects of the exploding German patrol boat, combined with hitting the river at speed. "Good work sir. Feel free to join the Royal Navy whenever it suits."

"Thanks, but it's not over yet and I am sick of that spy," he said pointing at the tall blond woman lobbing grenades at the freighter.

"Message from the Bobby Jean, sir," the radio operator said to the captain. "The destroyer is dodging torpedoes, so we need to take care of the fishing boat."

"What are your orders, Lieutenant Commander?" Henderson asked Butler.

"Attack," Butler replied simply, with anger in his voice. The crew on the CMB went back to battle stations and the captain pushed the throttle forward.

"I am going to stay bow on Mr. Butler," the captain said explaining the tactical plan. "That fishing boat will be no match for the Vickers once we get into range." Butler agreed and retrieved his hunting rifle to join the fight. He rested the high-powered weapon on top of the CMB's windscreen and took aim.

From the deck of the Bobby Jean, Donovan and Owens watched the next phase of the battle unfold. "What do you think Bill?" Owens asked Donovan.

"I wish the Charlotte were still on station Nash. It would make the job much easier. But we seem to be doing everything the hard way on this mission."

"Agreed," Owens replied. "But I will put my money on Dean and the CMB," he said confidently.

The men ducked as a grenade exploded forward on the main deck, taking out a wooden pallet stacked with bags of potatoes. There would be no french fries on the voyage home.

"I hope so Nash." Donovan replied as the men collected themselves from the first grenade to find its mark. "If whatever she is firing hits the bridge it will be game over. This freighter is not built for gun play."

* * *

Encouraged by the direct hit, Schuyler was now locked in and ready to kill. The Germans narrowed the distance between the fishing boat and the Bobby Jean, and Schuyler adjusted the grenade launcher to the required angle to take out the ship's bridge.

She fired another grenade at the Bobby Jean, again forcing the crew on the bridge, including Donovan and Owens to duck for cover. The grenade hit well forward of the bridge, exploding on the steel deck, and leaving a large dent, but failing to penetrate to the substructure below.

Seeing the CMB charging, Schuyler ordered the German soldier to put more fire on the CMB. He took aim with the hunting rifle and began firing at the British launch, but it was running bow on at full speed and almost impossible to target accurately.

"Let her have it with the Vickers," Butler ordered.

He fired his hunting rifle at the German spy but had the same problem as the German soldier. The speed of the CMB made it difficult to target the German's accurately and the bullet went wide right, hitting the back of the wheelhouse.

The Vickers opened-up and strafed the water along the port side of the fishing boat, narrowly missing the vessel but gaining the attention of the German spy.

"Destroy that launch!" a frustrated Schuyler again ordered the German soldier. The youngster was doing his best but the swells in the Congo River and speed of the CMB were doing him no favours.

The Vickers crew, on the other hand, was quickly finding its mark as the machine gun was screwed onto the deck and much more stable. The gun crew ripped a path of destruction along the side of the fishing boat, causing the German helmsman to take evasive action, which in turn knocked Schuyler off balance just as she let loose with the next grenade. She fell backwards as she pulled the trigger. The grenade went straight up, hitting the exterior wooden awning of the fishing boat above her, and exploding on impact.

The grenade ripped a hole in the awning and showered Schuyler with splinters leaving her a bloodied mess. The concussion from the blast also knocked her unconscious. The soldier with the rifle fell overboard as he lost his balance ducking the blast, while the helmsman, being forward of the explosion and in the relative safety of the wheelhouse, was unharmed. He needed no encouragement and turned the now smoldering fishing boat around and fled towards the Atlantic at full speed. He had no stomach for a fight with the well-armed patrol boat.

"Cease fire captain," Butler ordered as he watched the Germans turn tail and run. "Let them go. We are not at war, as I am constantly reminded," he said with a disappointed look on his face. He desperately wanted to finish the job, but that would have to wait for another day.

"To the Bobby Jean please captain," Butler ordered.

CHAPTER THIRTEEN

FANATICS EVERYWHERE

Watching the apparent failure of the German espionage effort from the bridge of the Hildebrand, the freighter's helmsman Oscar Kornheizer shook his head in disgust. Kornheizer, only nineteen years old, was just over six feet, lean, with blue eyes, curly black hair and a determined outlook on life. He had grown up in the era after the Great War and witnessed his mother, a widow, struggle to feed his two older sisters and himself.

He wanted to be the man of the household but was young and getting a job in the merchant navy, which he did the day he turned sixteen, was the best way of supporting his family. The youngster was a member of the Hitler Youth and had volunteered to join the Kriegsmarine, the German navy, just prior to the Hildebrand departing Hamburg. He hated how Germany had been treated by the rest of Europe after the Great War and was determined to do everything he could to support the Fatherland in its attempt to even the score.

He was joined on the bridge by the ship's engineer, Klaus Heinrich, who delivered the news that the propellers were repaired, and the ship could depart Matadi at their convenience. The explosives had not done as much damage as the captain had originally feared and the machine shop managed to straighten and patch them.

"Do you want me to test them, Klaus?" Kornheizer asked.

"Yes, fire up the engines and make sure they are spinning correctly." The engineer confirmed.

Kornheizer instructed the engine room to start the engines and he put the ship in gear. The propellers duly started spinning and the large container ship started to nudge along the wharf straining the ropes tying her to the dock. The repairs seemed to be holding.

"They sound good Klaus." Kornheizer complemented the engineer after a few seconds of testing. "There are no vibrations that would indicate they have not been properly repaired."

"Good. Let's pick up the captain and executive officer," Heinrich ordered his young colleague. He could see the two men bobbing in the harbor, apparently unharmed from their attempt at maritime suicide.

Heinrich went on deck and instructed the crew to cut the lines and make ready for immediate departure.

The youngster navigated the Hildebrand into the main harbor with his eyes set on the two officers who were treading water and looking quite helpless. The British had no interest in helping the sailors and Schuyler was running for her life. All show and no go, he thought to himself, of the Abwehr spy.

* * *

"Keep your eye on the screen, sailor," Billingsley ordered his sonar operator as the Charlotte searched for the German submarine. "No surprises please."

"Aye, aye sir," the operator said, studying the empty screen and watching the green arrow circle the monitor like a second hand on a watch.

Billingsley went on deck where his senior officer Stanley Johnson was scanning the horizon with his binoculars.

"Anything to report Stan?" Billingsley asked.

"No sign of the sub captain," he replied. "We have extra lookouts posted. She either escaped or is playing possum."

The captain retreated to the bridge wondering if the sub had given the destroyer the slip. He doubted it, and like his senior officer, suspected the U-Boat was sitting quietly, waiting for the Charlotte to give up the chase. For now, the game of cat and mouse was favouring the mouse.

* * *

While the Hildebrand's crew was rescuing their officers, the Bobby Jean was finally about to start her slow trek to the coast with the assistance of a tugboat.

Matadi was the final inland port up the mighty Congo River that could accommodate merchant shipping. A few kilometres upstream were the Yallala Falls, a series of waterfalls and rapids that acted as a natural impediment to commercial shipping. The tug would need to pull her about five kilometres to the river mouth and the relative safety of the open sea. The American destroyer would hopefully be waiting once it dealt with the German submarine. While the river could accommodate freighter traffic, it was too shallow for the much larger and heavier destroyer.

Butler and the crew on the CMB had docked alongside the Bobby Jean as it was preparing to leave the dock. They were waiting for Donovan and Owens to join their American colleague.

As the two Americans were about to depart the freighter for the patrol boat, Owens spotted the Hildebrand exit its birth and manoeuvre into the channel. "Bill, it looks like the Germans are up to something," Owens said raising the alarm to his boss.

"So they are," Donovan replied warily, watching the Hildebrand, and wondering what was coming next.

The Americans decided to stay with the Bobby Jean, doubting the Hildebrand was intending to leave peacefully.

Donovan took his binoculars and watched the German freighter manoeuvre slowly towards the middle of the channel. "It appears as if she is going to pick up the drowning rats," he said to Owens as he moved the binoculars between the Hildebrand and the two seamen bobbing in the river.

"Yes, it looks that way. What do you think?" Owens said to Donovan.

"I don't know, which is concerning," Donovan replied. He walked to the stern and called down to Butler who was waiting for the men in the CMB. "Dean. Keep an eye on the Hildebrand. If she makes any move to interrupt the

Bobby Jean's passage, open fire. Owens and I will stay on board until we are clear of the Germans."

"Roger Bill," Butler yelled back as he turned around to see what was happening with the Hildebrand.

Seeing for himself that the Hildebrand was moving into the channel he ordered Henderson to get the CMB to battle stations and stay between the two freighters. A few seconds later the patrol boat roared off and assumed position off the Bobby Jean's starboard side as the freighter was now clear of the dock and moving into the main channel. If the Hildebrand tried anything she would need to get past the British patrol boat to do it.

Butler waved to the Bobby Jean once they were in position. He was secretly hoping the Germans would do something stupid. He was in his element and loved every minute of the action.

* * *

The German U-Boat was running short of oxygen and would soon need to surface to recharge her batteries as well as take on fresh air as carbon dioxide levels were reaching dangerous levels. The captain was waiting for dusk to give him the necessary cover of darkness, but he no longer had the luxury of time. The sonar was showing the American warship running a circular pattern around the sub, indicating it knew roughly, but not exactly, where U-073 was hiding.

On the bridge of the Charlotte, Billingsley's hackles were up, and he decided it was time to change tactics. He knew the Germans could not hide forever and would soon need to get moving or surface. He didn't think the submarine had given him the slip as the much faster destroyer would easily run the sub down once it had a sonar contact, the lack thereof being a firm indicator that the sub was hiding and biding its time.

"Get depth charges ready," he ordered his executive officer, deciding on an aggressive course of action. "Let's run a vertical pattern, due south to due north, bisecting our current patrol route. The sub is in that circle somewhere so let's cut it in half."

"If that doesn't work, then we'll cut it in quarters."

"Aye captain," the executive officer acknowledged. The ship went into action as the helmsman swung the destroyer to ten degrees, and the crew, still on battle stations, readied the charges.

The Charlotte started spitting depth charges off its stern. The captain's assessment of the likely location of the U-Boat was spot on.

Coming under fire forced the captain of U-073 to blink.

"Ahead flank speed. Due south." Jaanzen ordered coolly. The sub sprang into life.

"They have us bracketed." He said calmly.

He did not know the destroyer was on a fishing expedition. The crew fired up the engines and the sub was soon making flank speed, trying to put distance between it and the destroyer. At worse the captain hoped that it would pull the destroyer off its patrol route, forcing its captain to decide between chasing the sub, or waiting for the freighter to emerge from the Congo. If it was the latter, then the sub would survive to fight another day.

A depth charge exploded above the sub, and then another off its port side. The crew instinctively ducked and held onto to anything they could find to steady their balance, as the sub structure of the vessel shook violently.

"Contact captain!" the Charlotte's sonar operator called out. "We are almost on top of her. About a hundred metres off our stern sailing south. We must have hit her with the first round of depth charges."

Needing no encouragement, Billingsley ordered the destroyer to do a U-turn. It quickly caught up with the sub and resumed depth charging. U-073 was in trouble.

"Sheisse," Jaanzen uttered, knowing he had blinked too quickly and put his ship and crew at risk of a gruesome death. "Dive helmsman. Set depth at one hundred metres then all ahead stop." One hundred metres was her maximum rated depth. He hoped the depth charges would explode above the sub and the destroyer would run past his ship, giving him a window to escape.

The sub dropped like a rock as it tried to evade the destroyer. All hands waited quietly, self-consciously looking up towards the ocean surface knowing the depth charges were coming down from above. The ploy failed and within a few minutes U-073 was again rocked, the underwater bombs exploding on either side of the submarine.

On the deck of the Charlotte, Billingsley watched the depth charges spitting off the stern like flyballs at a baseball practice. They were right on top of the sub, and he knew it. He would not stop until the target was destroyed. Satisfied that his munitions crew was getting on with the job he returned to the deck to check the sonar.

Knox had issued shoot-first orders, war, or no war, and he intended to press the advantage. It was obvious President Roosevelt was in no mood to put up with German aggression. It was also helpful that if the submarine went to its grave there would be no visible evidence that Germany could point to.

"Sir," An excited Johnson rushed onto the bridge. "Debris off the stern, about fifty metres."

Billingsley and Johnson went on deck for a look. There was oil leaking up to the surface with bits of flotsam mixed in the slick. They had hit their target.

"Ok Stan. Keep up the depth charges. Let's take no chances in case it is a ruse," Billingsley ordered Johnson.

"Aye, aye sir."

They need not have. The sub went down losing all hands. A depth charge punched a large hole in the port side of U-073 filling the cabin with water and sentencing the crew of the submarine to a watery grave. There was no chance of escape, or for the sub to surface and surrender.

U-073 had also failed to make radio contact with Canaris or the Kriegsmarine, so only the Americans knew her fate.

After an hour, with darkness approaching and no sonar signature from the U-Boat, the Charlotte cruised back to the river mouth. It would take her about an hour to get back on station. She would wait for the Bobby Jean five kilometres off the west coast of the Belgian Congo and assist Donovan's team as required.

* * *

Back at the port, two seamen dropped a net over the side of the Hildebrand. Heitz and Schultz scrambled up the side of the freighter and were helped on deck by two crewmen.

"Well, we are alive Schultz," the relieved captain said jovially to his executive officer, giving him a hug.

"What are your orders?" young Kornheizer asked his officers as he updated them on the state of the Hildebrand. "The ship is repaired; the tanks are full, and she can make eighteen knots."

Heitz nodded, saying nothing as he mulled over his options, and what, if anything, he could or should do to intercept the uranium. After a moment, he asked Schultz, "Well, what do you think? We have done our best and survived the effort but failed in our mission," he said, pointing out the obvious.

"With respect captain," Schultz started, "our job was to deliver the uranium once it was on board. Our colleagues at the Abwehr failed the Fatherland, and it is they who will be held accountable by the Führer."

"Maybe Schultz, but I doubt it," Heitz said fatalistically, being older and wiser, and having been on the receiving end of finger pointing in the past.

Young Kornheizer cleared his throat indicating he had something to say.

"Yes, mister Kornheizer. You might as well join the discussion. We are looking for ideas," Heitz said encouraging the youngster.

"Well captain, we are all in agreement that we we have no ability to take over the American ship or even damage it. We have no heavy weapons so we cannot get into a

- 225 -

shooting match with them," the youngster said, working through the situation. "And in any event, the British patrol boat is in our way.

"But equally, for five more kilometres the Americans are dependent on the tugboat to get the freighter down the channel to the river mouth. Without the tug she will not make it. She is too heavy, and the channel is too narrow. She will either run aground on a sand bar or stall."

Heitz continued the youngster's thought process. "And if we were to disable the tug, she would be dead in the water. And better yet, if we could sink the tug in the middle of the passage, the Americans could not exit the port. They would be stuck here," he said identifying the seed of a plan.

Kornheizer added another option. "Why don't we ram the tug and sink both ourselves and the tug? That would close the channel for months. What is the worst the Belgians can do to us? Throw us in jail for a few weeks until the Führer frees us?"

Heitz looked at Schultz. "What do you think?"

Schultz agreed. "We should try it. If we succeed, we will stop the uranium from going to the Americans. And if we fail, at least the Führer will know we tried everything in our power. It is our duty and the best way to save our skins if the worse happens," he concluded pragmatically, referring more to the prospect of facing retribution in Germany, rather than the wrath of the Americans, Brits or colonial Belgians.

All the men nodded in agreement, so Heitz issued the command. "Get us to full speed and issue weapons to the men. The target is the tugboat. Schultz, we have four boxes of explosives left. Get them rigged and ready to explode. We will need to put a hole in our hull once we ram the tug."

"Aye captain," Schultz said and went to the engine room to do the needful.

"Young Kornheizer. You have the helm. Run down that tug and make it fast," the captain said, slapping the youngster on the back.

"Aye captain!" Kornheizer said proudly, knowing he was contributing to the battle. He pushed the engines to full speed and maneuvered the Hildebrand into a crash course with the tug.

* * *

Butler and Henderson were both keeping a keen eye on the Hildebrand. "Captain, keep the Vickers ready in case we need to use it."

"The Germans are persistent bastards," Butler conceded showing the merchant seaman respect some for their efforts. His gut was telling him the Germans were going to make another attempt at either taking the Bobby Jean or sabotaging her efforts to get out of the channel and safely to sea.

"Raise the Bobby Jean please radioman," Butler ordered. It was time to talk to Donovan.

"Donovan here," the American said, taking the handset from the radio operator.

"Bill, this is Dean. Any idea what the Germans are up to?" he asked, hoping Donovan had a crystal ball.

"No, but you can be sure they are trying to get in our way," Donovan reasoned. "Their only options are to ram either us or the tugboat. If they sink the tug or stick a hole in our side, we will be stuck here."

"Can you get the Charlotte to stick a couple of shells across her bow?" Butler asked. "It might be enough to discourage her."

"I will ask Dean, but when she last reported she was out chasing a German sub and I don't know if she will get back in time," Donovan explained. "We cannot wait for her, so put some rounds into the Hildebrand with the machine gun. Hopefully, that will dissuade her crew from getting in our way."

"Roger that Bill," Butler confirmed, signing off.

* * *

Kornheizer had the Hildebrand positioned between the tug and the Bobby Jean. They were approximately one hundred fifty hundred metres from the tug and would catch her in about ten minutes while the American ship was still in the main channel.

The executive officer was back on the bridge updating Heitz. "Captain, the charges are set on top of the fuel tanks. She will go up like a rocket when she explodes," Schultz said grimly.

"Set the timer for ten minutes, arm the crew and ready the lifeboat," Heitz ordered. "Once we are fifty metres from the tug start the timer and get the lifeboat over the side. I will make sure she stays on course to ram the tug. I will jump and swim for it before the charges go off," he explained.

"Don't forget to pick me up," the captain said, winking at Schultz, trying to bring some levity to the tension filled situation.

"Don't worry captain," Schultz said smiling sympathetically. "We'll come for you."

Heitz returned the smile, albeit with a look of resignation on his face knowing that doing his duty could cost him his life. "Good. Now send an SOS to the ambassador and tell him to get someone pick us up at the port office, so we can hide out at the embassy before the Belgian authorities arrest us."

"Hopefully, the Americans will be graceful in defeat and let us escape," Heitz said optimistically albeit without conviction. As he spoke a shell crashed into the harbor fifty metres in front of them. The Charlotte was back on station.

"Shit. They are serious Schultz. Evasive action helmsman!" the captain instructed Kornheizer, as they ducked for cover. The young helmsman put the Hildebrand into a zigzag, hoping to avoid a fatal blow before they crashed into the tug.

The destroyer had arrived back at the mouth of the Congo and was lobbing shells at the German freighter. As the shelling began Butler ordered Henderson to begin the chase. The helmsman put the stick down, and the five hundred horsepower Sunbeam aircraft engine easily pushed the CMB to thirty knots, as the patrol boat rumbled towards its prey.

"Stand by, gunner," Butler yelled over the noisy twelve-cylinder beast. The machine gunner and loader took up position in the bow. The Vickers was on a tripod screwed into the deck and surrounded by sandbags. They were ready for action.

* * *

Back on the Hildebrand the captain watched, thinking through his strategy, as the British patrol boat ran straight towards them. He ordered his crew to fire on the British vessel before abandoning ship, and they set about their task enthusiastically. Another shell shattered the river, saturating the crew with fresh water from the mighty Congo. The Charlotte had the range locked in and three or four more shells could prove fatal. While a sturdy vessel, the Hildebrand was not designed to withstand many hits from twelve-pound shells.

"To the port side men," Heitz called through the ship's loudspeaker system. "Fire at will."

The crew needed no encouragement. They were only a hundred metres from the tug and would only need to survive the next five minutes. Then it would be game over for these men, or so they hoped. They opened fire on the patrol boat with their bolt action rifles.

A burst from the Vickers .303 air-cooled machine gun returned the favour with interest. The Vickers ripped a path of damage along the side of the Hildebrand forcing the crew to duck for cover. Bullets shattered the windows on the bridge with shards of glass hitting young Kornheizer in the hip, leaving him bloodied and grimacing in pain.

Seeing the youngster taking shrapnel the captain yelled encouragement to the youth to stay at his post and continue its pursuit of the tug. "Only a few more minutes Oskar. We cannot miss."

The race was on, either the Charlotte and the British patrol boat would hit the mark, or the Hildebrand would savage the tug and set off an explosion that would sink both ships and block the channel.

* * *

With the Germans' plan now in clear view, Donovan instructed Prentice to cut the tow lines and order the tug to take evasive action. The Bobby Jean's radio operator needed no encouragement. He was on the radio before his captain spoke and told the tug to make tracks and get out of the way of the Hildebrand.

The tug was also not waiting around. As soon as the lines were cut, she started to zigzag, engaging in a high stakes game of chicken with the Germans.

Donovan got on the radio to Butler. "Dean, give them another burst and try to turn them away from the tug."

"Aye, aye Bill," Butler said as he put his arm in the air and waved his hand in a circular fashion which was the signal for another attack.

The CMB was in position about fifty metres off the port side of the Hildebrand, protecting the Bobby Jean from whatever the Germans had in mind.

"Let's get moving captain," Butler yelled over the engines. "Give her another burst."

The helmsman put the throttle down and they headed for their prey.

The machine gunner strafed the port side again, but this time there was no response from the Hildebrand's crew. Butler could not see the starboard side of the freighter where the crew had retreated and were now climbing into the lifeboat ready to abandon ship. The last to join them was Kornheizer, who was limping noticeably from the glass shard protruding from his hip.

* * *

Another shell screamed over top of the Hildebrand, missing the stern by less than ten metres. The captain, now alone on deck, took evasive action turning hard to his port side as he tried to outguess the Charlotte's gunnery crew, as well as forcing the patrol boat off its line.

He looked over the starboard side of the freighter and could see the lifeboat was in the water and moving away from the Hildebrand. He took a deep breath, relieved knowing his crew was safe. He set the Hildebrand back online to ram the tug.

While the tug was taking evasive action, she was old and slow and not designed to maneuver or win a race. She was a tortoise and would be no match for the Hildebrand, which relatively speaking was the hare in the race. The German freighter was sitting high in the water, her hold empty and was quickly closing the distance between the two ships.

Unfortunately for the Hildebrand, the gunner on the Charlotte guessed right and aimed to the port side of the freighter. The shell hit the Hildebrand, exploding just off amidships, near the stern. The shell ripped through the deck and penetrated to the engine room, destroying the boiler, igniting the fuel tank, and setting off a massive blast as the explosives also combusted. The fireball was spectacular.

With a massive hole in her hull, and a fire out of control, the captain could now only save his own skin as the ship started to settle to the bottom of the river. He struggled with the concussion caused by the blast, which was making his head spin, and causing his vision to be blurred. Blood was trickling out of his ears, and he had lost his sense of balance.

He collapsed to the floor of the bridge, which was noticeably hot from the fire below. Trying to regain his feet the severe vertigo prevented him from finding his balance. Feeling faint he again fell to the floor, hitting it hard and losing consciousness. He would go down with the ship not knowing if the mission had succeeded.

CHAPTER FOURTEEN

NO RUBBER NECKING

"Woooow…" Butler said aloud, watching the fireworks in the distance. The CMB had left the action before the freighter was lit up by the Charlotte.

He was amazed at the damage a single shell could cause. It certainly was not a textbook explosion from the Navy munitions manual. He had no idea that the crew had packed the Hildebrand with explosives, which went off when the 12-pounder hit the engine room.

"Better steer clear captain," Butler said, ordering the captain to give the burning wreck a wide berth. Henderson swung the CMB south, towards the riverbank, and sped towards the Bobby Jean, missing the burning wreck by fifty metres.

On the bridge of the Bobby Jean, Captain Prentice instructed the tug to join up and resume towing the freighter, making sure they would get safely past the sinking

Hildebrand. The Americans were at risk of getting stuck in the main channel if the German freighter sank in front of them. The crew of the tug threw lines to the crew of the Bobby Jean and within a few minutes had resumed towing the freighter to the river mouth.

"Steady mister," Prentice said to his helmsman. "We need to get past that hull before it sinks."

"Aye, captain," the helmsman replied. "We should be able to get by. At least she is not sitting in the middle of the channel."

"Then full ahead mister. Let's not hang around rubber necking!" The captain ordered.

"Will we get through?" Donovan asked Prentice.

"We should do as long as nothing else explodes," Prentice replied nervously. "Given the size of the explosion, the German freighter must have been loaded with explosives and was going to take both herself and the tug to the bottom of the harbor. If both went down, we would have been stuck here."

"Sometimes it's better to be lucky than good, captain." Donovan said, repeating De Suter's prophetic words a few days previously. He went out on deck to join Owens who was conversing with Butler as the patrol boat had pulled alongside. They all marveled at the sight of the German freighter engulfed in flames.

Butler piped up. "Do you want us to give the crew a tow Bill?" The crew of the Hildebrand, excepting the captain, had survived the explosion, and were making good time rowing towards the port office.

"No. I will ask Goma to get the local police to look after them. They can sit in jail here for the next few months, so no one reports back to Hitler that one of his ships is missing. I will also get Goma to have Schuyler arrested if she steps outside the embassy grounds, assuming she is still alive," he said with a smile on his face. "If nothing else it will piss her off having to sit in a stinking cell waiting for her Führer to cut a deal with King Leopold. Now stand by, Nash and I will join you and follow the Bobby Jean out to sea," Donovan said as the freighter passed by the burning hull of the Hildebrand. She was now safely under control of the tug and on her way to the river mouth.

"Safe journey captain," Donovan said to the captain of the Charlotte as he declared their part of the mission complete.

"Likewise, Mr. Donovan. We will be in the Azores in eight days all going smoothly, and Knox is organizing another destroyer to meet us there for the trip across the Atlantic," Billingsley said, laying out their itinerary.

The Bobby Jean slowed down to let Owens and Donovan climb down the cargo net to join Butler on the CMB.

The CMB did a U-turn and pointed the patrol boat back up-river to Matadi. Captain Henderson put the stick down and the boat was soon doing thirty knots. The massive girth of the river near its mouth, and its placid surface, made it easy and pleasurable to travel back up the river.

The three Americans took a seat in the stern of the launch and enjoyed the ride.

* * *

That evening Donovan, Owens and Butler enjoyed a celebratory drink at the Sabena Hotel. Creighton and

Parker-Biggs joined them. It had been a long few days, and the men were looking forward to relaxing and getting a good night's sleep.

"Gentlemen! Please join us," Donovan called cheerfully to his British colleagues as they appeared in the garden. The waiter was following close behind the Brits carrying a bottle of Billecart Salmon champagne in an ice bucket.

Creighton and Parker-Biggs sat down to enjoy the festivities. Donovan updated Creighton on the clash between the Charlotte and the German U-Boat.

Creighton moved onto happier communications. "You have been mentioned in dispatches, Mr. Donovan and team," Creighton said as he took possession of a glass of champagne which was bubbling away in a Marie Antoinette flute. He handed the cable to Donovan.

"A well done from the President gentlemen," Donovan said reading the cable to Butler and Owens. "When you get back to Belgium make sure you put in for danger pay!"

"Thank you, sir, although I think Dean does this kind of thing for sport," Owens said cheerfully, raising his glass to toast his comrade in arms.

"It's harder than it looks Nash," Butler replied with a smile, looking at his glass of champagne and wishing it were beer.

"The Belgian colonial police were waiting for the crew of the Hildebrand as they got off the lifeboat, and Goma rescued the German who had fallen over the side of the fishing boat," Donovan said updating Creighton and Biggs. "They will sit on ice while the diplomats argue about their release. No sign of the spy however."

"The Belgians are going to keep an eye on the German embassy as she is probably holed up there. If she is travelling on a diplomatic passport, she will be free to leave the country." Donovan continued, tidying up the loose ends for the British SIS agents.

"There is one more piece of news…" Creighton began grimly. "Hitler has invaded Poland. And in compliance with His Majesties' treaty obligations with Poland, Britain as well as our European allies are now in a state of war with Germany."

The three Americans let out a collective whistle knowing that the world had suddenly changed, and global conflict could no longer be avoided. It was here and now.

Biggs piped up, trying to look on the bright side. "And I have been posted to Paris gentlemen. The Foreign Office is worried that the French may not be up for a war with the Nazis, so they are beefing up the diplomatic efforts to get our wine-loving friends ready for the inevitable."

"Given the circumstances gentlemen, I think we have at least given our allies a head start," Donovan said, thinking through the ramifications of the Nazis building a bomb with the Congolese uranium.

"Well said Bill," Creighton replied. "But I dare say Hitler will not be put off by our efforts. I hope we do not have to work together in the future, but I cannot say that with any confidence," he concluded with a typical understatement.

* * *

Donovan returned to the United States two weeks later, taking the reverse journey of the trip south. He parted company with Owens, Butler, and Parker-Biggs in Lisbon. They enjoyed a raucous evening before going their separate ways, each dragging along an alcohol-induced headache. This time they were careful to avoid the bar at the Estoril hotel.

Donovan was summoned to the White House by President Roosevelt, and he duly arrived on the 22nd of September 1939. He was greeted at the entrance to the West Wing by Admiral Knox, and they walked down the long corridor to the Oval Office where Roosevelt and Cordell Hull were waiting.

"Good morning, Bill," a chirpy Roosevelt said as he greeted Donovan. "Please take a seat."

Donovan sat on the sofa with Knox and Hull as the President kicked the meeting into gear. "Well done on the matter in the Congo, Bill," President Roosevelt said cheerfully. "There will be a citation in it for you. For now, we need to keep the operation a secret in case my political adversaries get wind of the scrap with the Germans."

"No problem, Mr. President," Donovan replied. "Formal recognition is not necessary. You know I do these jobs out of my love for my country."

"Nevertheless Bill, you will be recognized when we are ready for such things," the President said, knowing that the United States owed a great debt to him, as well as Owens and Butler. "Bill. I need you to join me full time," Roosevelt said, getting to the point of the meeting.

"What do you have in mind Mr. President?"

"I am convinced that the United States will be dragged into war with Germany at some point, and I would also not be surprised if Japan entered the conflict. I want you to join my staff in the Executive Office, Bill," the President said, his recruiting pitch now well underway. "I want you to be an ad hoc adviser on international matters, and in particular matters pertaining to security. A national security adviser if you will."

Hull interjected. "Bill, the State Department can't be seen to be undertaking the kind of job you did in the Belgian Congo, but both the President and I believe these missions will come up more frequently now the world has moved to a war footing."

"The Brits have their SIS," Roosevelt continued. "I expect we will need to set up our own intelligence network at some point soon, and we want to be ready when the time comes. I want you to work with me to get the framework for such an organization established."

"And then if needed, I want you to be our point man on specific international issues." He continued, referring to projects like repatriating the uranium from the Congo.

"Mr. President," Donovan said proudly. "It will be my honor."

"Good Bill. Can you start Monday?" Roosevelt asked seriously.

And with that Donovan joined the White House team as they got ready to fight a war they were not yet fighting.

EPILOGUE

The United States would be a bystander at the beginning of the second world war, not entering the conflict until after the Japanese attack on Pearl Harbour on 7 December 1941, and the subsequent declaration of war on the United States by Germany and Italy three days later. The Americans needed time to prepare for war, due in part to a lack of firepower caused by many years of neglecting its armed forces as well as an isolationist foreign policy.

By executive order, President Roosevelt would establish the Office of Strategic Services in June 1942, appointing Donovan to head the new spy agency. One of Donovan's first acts would be to appoint Owens and Butler as senior OSS agents and the three would take on a number of important missions during the war.

In the meantime, and with war starting in Europe, Owens and Butler returned to their posts in Belgium not knowing where they would end up, particularly if, and when, the United States entered the conflict. For now, they enjoyed diplomatic immunity as their country was a neutral.

Neutrality would serve the men well, particularly in 1940 when Hitler invaded Denmark and Norway, followed a month later when France, Belgium, and Holland met the same fate. Their immunity would give them flexibility to help their allies with little fear of repercussions from the murderous Nazis. They would be directed by Donovan, through the Office of the President, to help the allied cause, engaging in several covert missions.

Parker-Biggs on the other hand, needed to be more careful. With the United Kingdom declaring war on Germany following the Nazi invasion and occupation of Poland, he was a wanted man. He was a known spy and would be shot if caught in German-controlled territory. Paris would be peaceful enough for the next seven months but that would end in May 1940 when German tanks bypassed the Maginot Line and forced France to surrender in the most embarrassing of circumstances.

Owens, Butler, and Parker-Biggs would stay in touch and their relationship would be put to the test in June 1940 when the Nazis took up residence in Paris.

Creighton remained at his position in the Belgian Congo but would be posted to Alexandria a few months later. His Majesty needed seasoned professionals in strategic locations, and Creighton's talents would be tested in the coming months as station chief in Egypt. His work on the Congo matter impressed his superiors and moved his resume to the top of the promotions pile at MI-6. He would be followed to Alexandria by McInerney, as the British army was desperately in need of experienced officers to serve in the desert at the beginning of World War II. Henderson would also be on the move, as he would be put in charge of a squadron of motor torpedo boats in Malta.

On the German side, Schuyler would not make it back to Berlin until April 1940. It would take her six months, at a hospice in Munich, to recover from her concussion and wounds. The German embassy in Leopoldville manufactured a diplomatic passport for her and when she was well enough, she left on the first available flight. She managed to successfully blame Hofmayer for the mission's failure and would again work for Canaris as a senior agent.

The crew of the Hildebrand was not so lucky and would sit in the local jail in Leopoldville until January 1940 when the Nazis finally swapped them for two suspected Belgian spies. By the time they returned to Germany the war was well underway.

So, on the eve of World War II the joint mission of the United States and Britain to take control of the world's largest cache of Uranium-235 took on a much more strategic significance. The two nations had prevented the Germans early access to the fuel required to build a super weapon, Roosevelt had taken the decision to set up his own spy agency, and the Brits and Americans had established a good working relationship. How they would work together in Europe was about to be tested.

Mike Drogemuller's career has spanned public policy, corporate communications, consulting, writing and entrepreneurial endeavours. He grew up in Canada and moved to New Zealand together with his partner Jan, after graduating university. Following completion of a United Nations internship, he joined the New Zealand Department of Trade and Industry. Mike started his communications career in Wellington, before moving to Australia a few years later. His specialisation, both as a consultant and a senior corporate executive, was financial communications. He authored a range of documents including annual reports, prospectuses, corporate profiles and offering memorandums. Twenty-two years and twin boys later, they decided to return to Canada to bring up their young family, as well as helping their elderly parents. An enthusiastic amateur historian, Mike has studied World War II in detail and finally turned his hand to writing this fictional account, the author's first novel.

www.mikedrogemuller.com

LES COURSES – *The Errands* - the second book in the series reunites Donovan and his proteges Lieutenant Commander Dean Butler and diplomat Nash Owens in Paris at the onset of World War II, where together with their colleagues at MI-6 and the Duxieme Bureau, they must foil Nazi attempts to gain control of a large supply of heavy water. Look for the release of this WW2 spy thriller at your favourite bookseller in late 2022.

Operation 235: The Race for Uranium… tracks the power struggle between the United States of America and Germany… as the two nations battled for complete control of the world's purest uranium deposit. Set in the summer of 1939 as Europe prepares for the cusp of the largest war it has ever seen, we travel the globe to the Belgian Congo, where a cutthroat German intelligence ploy is underway to bring down America's finely planned operation to ship the uranium out.

It can be tricky to achieve an accurate balance of historical facts but also leave room for a novel to build its drama and tension, and Mike Drogemuller does exceptionally well in this engaging and informative historical novel. The key to his success is in his characters, who bring a layer of humanity to the complex political, economic and military goings-on as we see them puzzle the situation out on the ground, as well as struggle and suffer at the hand of their savvy and ruthless enemies. I especially enjoyed the stylization of the German Abwehr and their many inventive techniques of infiltration and attack. I recommend Operation 235 to all historical fiction fans…

— Reader's Favourite - 5 Stars

Printed in Great Britain
by Amazon